s
b
t
ba
T

A LEAN THIRD

ACKNOWLEDGEMENTS

Other than the collection *Lean Tales* (Jonathan Cape Ltd, London, 1985), a number of these stories first appeared, and in varying forms: <u>Busted Scotch</u>, <u>The Witness</u> and <u>learning the Story</u> were published in *Words*, 1977; <u>the same is here again</u> in *A.M.F.*, 1979; <u>In a betting shop to the rear of Shaftesbury Avenue</u> in the *Glasgow Magazine*, 1983; <u>Where I was</u> and <u>The City Slicker and The Barmaid</u> in *Three Glasgow Writers*, Molendinar Press, Glasgow, 1976; <u>Where I was</u> also in the *Fiction Magazine*, 1984; <u>Extra cup</u> (under the title <u>Mozambique</u>) in *Masque*, 1976; <u>Manufactured in Paris</u>, <u>The Place!</u> and <u>An Enquiry Concerning Human Understanding</u> in *Short Tales from the Night Shift*, Print Studio Press, Glasgow, 1978.

James Kelman

A Lean Third

with
an
afterword
by
the
author

Tangerine Press 2015

ISBN 978-0-9573385-6-2 (paperback)
     978-0-9573385-1-7 (hardback)

A LEAN THIRD. COPYRIGHT © 2014 JAMES KELMAN.
Reproduced by permission of the author c/o Rogers, Coleridge & White Ltd.,
20 Powis Mews, London W11 1JN
THIS EDITION FIRST PUBLISHED 2015 BY TANGERINE PRESS
18 RIVERSIDE ROAD
GARRATT BUSINESS PARK
LONDON
SW17 0BA
ENGLAND
eatmytangerine.com
PRINTED IN ENGLAND

Printed on 100% recycled, acid-free paper.

for
Agnes Owens and Alasdair Gray

Jim Kelman

Table of Contents

A LEAN THIRD

Busted Scotch

I had been looking forward to this Friday night for a while. The first wage from the first job in England. The workmates had assured me they played Brag in this club's casino. It would start when the cabaret ended. Packed full of bodies inside the main hall; rows and rows of men-only drinking pints of bitter and yelling at the strippers. One of the filler acts turned out to be a scotchman doing this harrylauder thing complete with kilt and trimmings. A terrible disgrace. Keep Right On To The End Of The Road he sang with four hundred and fifty males screaming Get Them Off Jock. Fine if I had been drunk and able to join in on the chants but as it was I was staying sober for the Brag ahead. Give the scotchman his due but — he stuck it out till the last and turning his back on them all he gave a big boo boopsidoo with the kilt pulled right up and flashing the Y-fronts. Big applause he got as well. The next act on was an Indian Squaw. Later I saw the side door into the casino section opening. I went through. Blackjack was the game until the cabaret finished. I sat down facing a girl around my own age, she was wearing a black dress cut off the shoulders. Apart from me there was no other punters in the room.

Want to start, she asked.

Aye. Might as well. I took out my wages.

O, you're scotch. One of your countrymen was on stage tonight.

That a fact.

She nodded as she prepared to deal. She said, How much are you wanting to bet?

I shrugged. I pointed to the wages lying there on the edge of the baize.

All of it . . .

Aye. The lot.

She covered the bet after counting what I had. She dealt the cards.

Twist.

Bust . . .

the same is here again

My teeth are grut.

What has happened to all my dreams is what I would like to know. Presently I am a physical wreck. If by chance I scratch my head while strolling showers of dandruff reel onto the paved walkway, also hairs of varying length. Tooth decay. I am feart to look into a mirror. I had forgotten about them, my molars; these wee discoloured bones jutting out my gums and lonely, neglected, fighting amongst themselves for each particle of grub I have yet to pick. Jesus. And my feet – and this mayhap is the worst of my plight – my feet stink. The knees blue the hands filthy the nails grimy, uneatable. What I must do is bathe very soon.

One certainty: until recently I was living a life; this life is gone, tossed away in the passing. I am washed up. The sickness burbles about in my gut. A pure, physical reaction at last. I feel it heaving down there, set to erupt – or maybe just to remain, gagging.

It is all a mystery as usual. I am very much afraid I am going off my head. I lie on pavements clawing at myself with this pleasant smile probably on the countenance. I have been this way for years. More than half my life to present has been spent in acquiring things I promptly dispose of. I seldom win at things. It is most odd. Especially my lack of interest. But for the smile, its well-being, the way I seem to regard people. It makes me kind of angry. I am unsure about much. Jesus christ.

Where am I again. London is the truth though I was reared in Glasgow. In regard to environment: I had plenty. But.

The weather. The hardtopped hardbacked bench concreted to the concrete patch amidst the grass. My spine against the hardback. My feet stuck out and crossed about the ankles. My testicles tucked between my thighs. I am always amazed no damage is done them. I have forgotten what has happened to the chopper. The chopper is upright though far from erect. It lies against the fly of my breeks. And now uncomfortable.

Explanations sicken me. The depression is too real. A perpeptual thirst but not for alcohol. Milk I drink when I find it. Smoking is bad. Maybe I am simply ill. Burping and farting. All sorts of wind. I should have a good meal of stuff. But even the thought. Jesus.

My hand has been bleeding. I cut it while entering a car. A stereo and one Johnny Cash cassette. My life is haunted by country & western music.

I have no cigarette in my gub.

And yet this late autumnal daylight. The spring in my step. Grinning all the while and wishing for hats to doff to elderly women. I am crying good-evening to folk. I might be in the mood for a game of something. Or a cold shower. When I settle down to consider a future my immediate straits are obliged to be conducive. I am grateful for the clement weather. Facts are to be faced. I am older than I was recently. And I was feart to show my face that same recently. Breakfast is an awful meal. If you dont get your breakfast that is you fucked for the day.

I cannot eat a Johnny Cash cassette.

Breakfast has always been the one meal I like to think I insist upon. When I have money I eat fine breakfasts. One of the best I ever had was right here in the heart of old London Town. A long time ago. So good I had to leave a slice of toast for appearances' sake. I was never a non-eater. Could always devour huge quantities of the stuff. Anything at all; greasy fried bread, burnt custard or eggs. Even with the flu or bad hangovers. A plate of soup at 4 in the morning. I cannot understand people scoffing at snails' feet and octopi although to be honest I once lifted a can of peasbrose from a supermarket shelf only to discover I couldnt stomach the bastarn stuff. So: there we are. And also food-poisoning I suppose. If I ever get food-poisoning I would probably not feel like eating. Apart from this

But not now. Not presently, and this is odd. My belly may have a form of cramp.

Immediately my possessions include money I shall invest in certain essentials as well as the washing of that pair of items which constitute the whole of my wardrobe in the department of feet viz my socks. For my apparel excludes pants and vest. An effect of this was my chopper getting itself caught in the zipping-up process that follows upon the act of pissing. Normally one is prepared for avoiding such occurrences. But this time, being up an alley off one of her majesty's thoroughfares, I was obliged to rush. ZZZIPPP. Jesus. The belly. Even the remembrance. For a couple of moments I performed deep breathing exercises aware that my next act would of necessity be rapid. And this was inducing vague associations of coronary attacks. My whole trunk then became icy cold. UUUNZZZIPP. Freed. It would not have happened had I been wearing pants. If I was being cared for pants would pose no problem, and neither would vests. Vests catch and soak up sweat unless they are made of nylon. In which case the sweat dribbles down your sides and is most damp and irritating.

My face looks to be ageing but is fine. A cheery face. It laughs at me from shop windows. The hairs protruding from my nostrils can be mistaken for the top of my moustache. The actual flesh, the cheekbones and red-veined eyeballs, the black patches round the sockets. Every single thing is fine. I am delighted with the lines. On my left – the right in fact, side of my nose has formed a large yellow head which I squeezed until the matter burst forth. I am still squeezing it because it lives. While squeezing it I am aware of how thin my skin is. I put myself in mind of an undernourished 87 year old. But the skin surrounding the human frame weighs a mere 6 ounces. Although opposed to that is the alsatian dog which leapt up and grabbed my arm; its teeth punctured the sleeve of the garment I was wearing but damage to the flesh was nil.

I bathed recently; for a time I lay steeping in the grime, wondering how I would manage out, without the grime returning to the pores in my skin. The method I employed was this: I arose in the standing position. The grime showed on the hairs of my legs though and I had to rinse those legs with cold because the hot had finished. I washed my socks on that occasion. They are of good quality. I sometimes keep them stuffed in the back pocket of my jeans.

The present is to be followed by nothing of account. Last night was terrible. All must now be faced. It has much to do with verges and watersheds.

Taxis to Blackfriars Bridge for the throwing of oneself off of are out of the question.

I have the shivers.

Reddish-blue blisters have appeared on the soles of my feet. They are no longer bouncing along. I can foresee. Nothing of account will follow. For some time now the futility of certain practices has not been lost on me. I shall sleep with the shivers, the jeans and the jumper, the socks and the corduroy shoes. I can forecast points A or point B: either is familiar. All will depend on X the unknown (which also affords of an either/or). The A and B of X equals the A and B that follow from themselves, not A and not B being unequal to not B and A. And they cannot be crossed as in Yankee Bets. Yet it always has been this way and I alone have the combinations.

I was planning on the park tonight. I left a brown paper bag concealed in a hedge near the Serpentine for the purpose. It will have been appropriated by now.

The trouble might well be sleep. I had a long one recently and it may well have upset the entire bodily functioning. This belly of mine. I must have slept for 10 hours. Normally I meet forenoons relatively alert.

Sheltering in an alley the other night, the early hours, in a motion-less state. I should have been smoking, had just realized the cigarette in my gub as not burning where it should have been burning. As I reached for a match I heard movement. Two cats were on the job less than 20 yards distant. The alley banked by high walls. The cats should have been free from spectators and yet here was me, jesus. In a film I saw recently there was this scruffy dog and a lady dog and he took her out for the night down this back alley to meet his friends and these friends of his were Chefs in an Italian Restaurant, one of whom was named Luigi if I remember correctly. He brought out a table and candlesticks and while the dogs sat down the other friend came out with an enormous quantity of spaghetti and stuff. While they were tucking in out came Luigi again with a stringed instrument and him and his pal began singing an operatic duet.

The grass grows in a rough patch and cannot have it easy. The blades are grey green and light green; others are yellow but they lie directly on the earth, right on the soil. My feet were there and the insects crawled all around. A fine place for games. They go darting through the green blades and are never really satisfied till hitting the yellow ones below. And they dart headlong, set to collide all the time into each other but no, that last-minute body swerve. And that last-minute body swerve appears to unnerve them so that they begin rushing about in circles or halting entirely for an approximate moment.

I have to clear my head. I need peace peace peace. No thoughts. Nothing. Nothing at all.

Here I am as expected. The shoulders drooping; they have been strained recently. Arms hanging, and the fingers. Here: and rubbing my eyes to open them on the same again. Here, the same is here again. What else.

The Glenchecked Effort

This jacket had a glencheck pattern and one back centre vent, two side pockets and one out breast welt, two inside pockets and one in-tick. It was made to fit a 40" chest and the arms of a 6' 4" gentleman. The buttons, two down the front and one on each cuff, were of dimpled leather. Inside the in-tick were ticket stubs and 4 spent matches. The inside pocket to the right contained a spotless handkerchief of the colour white, having parallel lines along the border. The left outside pocket held 18 pence in 2 pence pieces. It was a warm jacket. Handwoven in Harris read the label. It hung on a hook from where I lifted it neatly and stepped quickly outside and off. Though hanging loosely upon me it was a fine specimen and would have done much to protect me during the coming harsh winter. It should be stated that previous garments have afforded a more elegant finish but never before had I felt more pleasure than when surveying that person of mine while clad in the glenchecked effort.

I positioned myself to one corner of a rather quiet square to the right-hand side of Piccadilly looking south i.e. southwest. Two males and two femalesapproached, all four of whom were of the Occidental delineation; each pair of eyes was concealed behind medium-sized spectacles with darkened shades. Can you spare a bloke a bob? I asked.

Pardon …

Profferring my right hand in halting fashion I shrugged my shoulders, saying: A bob, can you spare a bloke a bob?

They were foreign. They conferred in their own language. At intervals I was obliged to glance to the ground when a gaze was directed towards me. I shuffled my feet. Then suddenly a handful of coins was produced and projected towards me. Many thanks, I said, many thanks. I clicked my heels, inclining my head. And off they went. Upon depositing the money into the left outside pocket I lowered myself to the pavement; folding my arms I sat on my heels and thus rested for several minutes. A discarded cigarette then appeared in close proximity to my shoes. Instantly I had collected it. I sucked the smoke deep into my lungs, managing to obtain a further three puffs before finally I was forced to chip it away towards the kerb. I reknotted my shoelaces and rose to the favoured standing position.

An elderly couple had entered my line of vision, the progress of each being considerably abetted by the instance of two fine Malacca canes. With a brief nod of appreciation I stepped hesitantly forwards. Can you spare a bloke a bob? I quoth.

With nary a sideways glance they hobbled past me, their canes striking the pavement in most forcible manner.

You sir, I cried to a youngish man, can you spare a bloke a bob?

What ...

Across the road I spied two uniformed fellows observing me with studied concentration. Slowly I turned and in a movement, was strolling to the corner, round which I hastened onwards. The skies were appearing to clouden. Yet my immediate prospects I continued to view with great optimism. Choosing a stance athwart a grassy verge I addressed successive pedestrians, but to no avail. A middle-aged couple had paused nearby, viewing my plight with apparent concern. Madam, quoth I, can you ...

You're a bloody disgrace, she said, that's what you are; giving us a showing up in front of the English.

I'm really most dreadfully sorry missis, I gave as my answer, I have been disabled.

That's no excuse for scrounging! She turned to her companion: Have you ever seen the like?

Missis, said I, I've a wife and two weans and I can assure you, having flitted down here in search of the new life I had the bad misfortune to fall off a roof.

And would you look at the state of that jacket he's wearing! he's lifted it from somewhere.

I have not.

Maybe he's genuine, hazarded her companion.

Ha ha.

I am missis, I really am.

Oh you are are you!

About to retort I inadvertently sneezed. I tugged the handkerchief from my pocket; out popped a membership card to the British Museum. You see, I said as I swabbed at my nostrils, here's my membership card to the British Museum; since my fall I've been embarking on a series of evening classes with a view to securing a light post.

I think he's genuine, the man remarked and withdrawing a 50 pence coin from a trouser pocket he handed it to me.

You're too soft, muttered the woman.

Now you're not letting me down? asked the man firmly.

Definitely not mister. Thanks a lot. I can assure you . . .

Not letting you down! cried the woman. Hh!

Come on Doreen, muttered the man then taking her by the arm, they continued on toward the very heart of the City. But I continued northwards. Soon I was entering the hallowed portals of our splendid literary museum. Moving briskly I proceeded beyond the lines of uniformed worthies at a pace I deemed seemly. Finding a more secluded room I occupied a chair at a table and settled for an indeterminate period. At length a bearded fellow who had been staring intently at the bibliographical pages of an handsomely bound volume, rose quietly and walked off. On the chair adjacent to his own lay an anorak, a plastic container, and a camera. Moments later I was strolling from the room, the camera safely secured in my inside left pocket. Entering a lavatory I continued to stroll, and passed into a vacant cubicle wherein I would remain for a lengthy interval. To occupy myself I examined each pocket and the gap between Harris Tweed and nylon lining, hoping against hope that I might discover other articles. It was not to be. Yet during my time in the cubicle no solitary voice of an excited nature had pierced my repose. There was much for which to be thankful. I counted to three then pulled the plug and promptly unsnibbed the cubicle door. With practiced eye I glanced to the washbasins before stepping forwards. I washed my hands. In the mirror I surveyed my glencheck jacket with undisguised satisfaction. Just then, as I prepared to dry my hands, an object attracted my attention. It was a knapsack. Slowly I turned, and in a movement, was strolling for the exit, uplifting the knapsack without the slightest check in my stride, and out through the doorway, allowing the door to swing backwards. In an instant I had considered the various uniformed gentlemen, their respective positions and demeanour, and was moving briskly, stepping into the magnificent surroundings of the vast entrance hall, then downwards onto the paved pathway to the iron gates, mingling with diverse individuals.

My getaway had been achieved with absurd ease. I was elated. You lucky bastard, I thought, you've knocked it off again!

The clouds were forming in puffs of the purest white. Surely a sign! Quickening my pace I crossed Russell Square, marching resolutely to the small grass park some two furlongs distant. While making my way to the rearmost bench my attention was drawn to a tearful urchin whose ball was ensconced on top of a thorny bush. I reached for it and gave it an almighty boot. The ball travelled high in the air. I patted the little fellow on the head and off he scampered in pursuit. When seated on the bench I sat for a time before examining the contents of the knapsack. But at last the moment had arrived; with a brief glance to the sky I tugged at the zip, and could list the following articles:

  (i) One pair socks of the colour navy blue
 (ii) One comb, plastic
(iii) One towel
 (iv) One pair swimming trunks of the colours maroon & white
  (v) One plastic bag containing: a] cheese sandwich
                                    b] lettuce & tomato sandwich
                                    c] slice of Madeira cake.

I smiled to myself and, withdrawing the camera from my inside left pocket, deposited it at the bottom of the knapsack. As I rose from the bench I chanced to glance at '... God's fair heaven', and was reminded of these few lines of the lyricist:

Tell me – What is the meaning of man,
Whence hath he come, whither doth go ...

Slinging the knapsack over my shoulders with a mischievous grin I walked onwards.

The Witness

As expected the windows were draped over with offwhite curtains, the body dressed in the navyblue three-piece suit, with the grey tweed bunnet on the head. Drawing a chair close in I sat smoking. I noticed the eyelids parting. The eyes were grey and white with red veins. The cigarette fell from my fingers. I reached quickly to get it up off the carpet. A movement on the bed. Scuffling noises. The head had turned. The eyes peering toward me. There was not a thing I could say. He was attempting to sit up now. He sat up. I placed a hand of mine on his right forearm. I was trying to restrain him. He wanted to rise. I withdrew my hand and he swivelled until his feet contacted space. I moved back. His feet lowered to the carpet then the rest of his body was up from the bed. He stood erect, the shoulders pushed back. The shoes on his feet; the laces were knotted far too tightly. I picked the grey tweed bunnet up from where it now was lying by the pillow and passed it to him, indicating his head. He took it and pulled it on, smoothed down the old hair at the sides of his head. I was wanting to know if he was going to the kitchen: he nodded. Although he walked normally to the door he fumbled on the handle. He was irritated by this clumsiness. He made way for me. I could open the door easily. He had to brush past me. The cuff of his right sleeve touched my hand. I watched him. When he got to the kitchen door he did not hesitate and he did not fumble with its handle. The door swung behind him. I heard her voice cry out. He was making for her. I gazed through the narrow gap in the doorway. He was struggling with her. He began to strike her about the shoulders, beating her down onto her knees; and she cried, cried softly. This was it. This was the *thing*. I held my head in both hands.

Are you drinking sir?

They had been seeking me for ages but being a devious old guy I managed to give them the slip on quite a few occasions. They found me in the broo. I was in there performing my song & dance routine, music from the first world war. At first I seemed not to notice them standing in the doorway then when I did I acted as though totally uninterested and my bravado had to be respected, not for its own sake so much as the effect it had on my pursuers. I turned my back on them and performed to those queuing to sign the register. Behind the counter the clerks looked slightly irritated although a couple of the younger brigade were smiling at my antics. But their smiles didnt linger, they continued working as though I wasnt there. I didnt bother at all, just carried on with the performance. Somehow an impression had been gained that no matter how erratically I might behave the clerks would never have me ejected. No doubt the reaction would have been different had I become violent, or even explicitly abusive. Then suddenly, towards the end of a song, I lost concentration for a moment and appeared in danger of failing to perceive the course – but then I grinned briefly and continued the game. It was strange to behold. Nearby there were four youths sitting on a bench and they were stamping their feet and cheering and then one of them had flicked a burning cigarette end in my direction. I was dancing so nimbly that I scarcely seemed to interrupt myself while bending to uplift it; I nipped off the burning ash, sticking the remainder of it in an interior pocket of my greatcoat. Then I glanced swiftly at the doorway, whirled to face the counter; onwards I jigged across the floor, wagging my right forefinger at two young girls queuing at Enquiries. I proceeded to address the chorus at them, the girls smiling their embarassment, laughing lightly that they had no money, nor even a cigarette to spare. Yet still I persisted at them and the girls now having to avert their faces from me while I with the beaming smile, cutting my capers as though the doorway had never existed. And thank you sir, I was crying to a smallish fellow who had rolled me a cigarette, thank you sir. This distracting me from the girls and back again I faced the counter; but my sly glance to the door was unmistakeable and I held the rolled cigarette aloft in my left hand, blatantly displaying it for their benefit. And I laughed at no one especially and again cried thank you sir, thank you sir, with both arms aloft now and waggling my hands round and round in preparation for the launch into my final chorus, but just at this point I made good my escape, and it wasnt till much later that again they found me. I was in a stretch of waste ground near the river. I stared at them when they approached, but the stare only expressed the vaguest curiosity. My head lolled sideways, knocking the unbuttoned epaulette askew. They came forward and prodded my shoulder until my eyelids parted and my groan became a groan of recognition. Thank you sir I muttered thank you sir, and them, stepping back the way as though alarmed. But they werent alarmed, they were angry. And judging by the manner in which my gaze dropped to the ground I was trying to avoid witnessing it. And then they began talking to me in a language that was foreign. At length they stopped. I withdrew a halfsmoked cigarette from an interior pocket and held it to my mouth until being given a light. I inhaled only once on it, before placing it carefully on the ground; then I picked it up and stubbed it out, smiling in a very sleakit way. I glanced at them and said are you drinking sir? For a moment there was silence. When they began shouting at me there was an odd sense in which it seemed to have lasted a while but only now become audible. But to none of it did I react. I was not smiling, I sat there as though in deep concentration. Eventually there was silence again, and they stared at me with open contempt. It was obvious I was now getting irritated. I looked at them and glared, my eyes twitching at the corners as though I was about to say something but I didnt say anything, I just shook my head and grunted sarcastically; it was being made plain that I couldnt care less. If there was a point for them it was now.

In a betting shop to the rear of Shaftesbury Avenue

Hey John! John . . . I grinned: How you doing?

He made to walk past me.

John, I said quickly, how's it going – I thought you were in Manchester?

What . . . He looked at me. My name's no John. He sniffed and glanced sideways, then muttered: McKechnie.

McKechnie! Christ. Aye . . . I thought you were in Manchester? How you doing man?

He looked away from me. I've no been in Manchester for years. And again he made to walk past me but I stepped slightly to the front.

Christ, so you left! I said.

Aye, years ago. He sniffed, gazed round the interior of the betting shop. It was a poky wee dump of a place and with nearly quarter of an hour till the first race only a couple of people were about. McKechnie watched them. He was holding a rolled newspaper in his left hand.

So how long you been here then? you been here long?

What . . . naw. He glanced up at the information board where a clerk had gone to scribble the names of the day's non-runners. He glanced across to the counter; the two women were eating sandwiches, sipping at cups of tea. Then he glanced back to me, and he frowned momentarily. He said: Mind that wife of mine? I'm in for a divorce off her. She wants the wean, but I'm getting the wean. Lawyer says I'm a certainty. And these lawyers know the score.

Aye.

He nodded.

After a moment I said, Aye – these lawyers!

He nodded again. The door opened and in came a punter, then another. McKechnie had noticed them and he moved a little. Soon after this came the first betting show of the day.

The other people were just hanging about, mainly staring at the formpages tacked onto the walls. On the information board the clerk was marking in the prices against listed runners. He held a fresh cigarette cupped in one hand. McKechnie unrolled his newspaper, turned a page.

So you left then? I said.

He nodded, without taking his gaze from the newspaper, not even raising his head. Then he shrugged, Aye, he said, I went to Sheffield.

Sheffield!

Mmhh.

Christ sake! I said. Sheffield! At this point a further betting show came through. When it was over I said again: Sheffield! Hh!

He only sniffed, still gazing at the racing pages.

Did you ever think of going back then? to Manchester I mean – did you never think of going back?

What … He barely shook his head, not looking at me, he grunted: Hard race this.

I shrugged. The favourite cant get beat, it's a good thing. Odds-on but. Odds-on look on, you know the old saying.

McKechnie frowned, rubbing at his chin; he pointed at the selection forecast by one of the racing journalists. That's what he says and all. I dont know but, I hate backing these odds-on shots too. It's one to beat it I want. He glanced back at me: Warrior Queen's supposed to be the only danger.

Aye, it's got a wee chance right enough. But … Heh, I said, d'you ever see Tommy on your travels?

Tommy?

Aye.

McKechnie's forehead wrinkled as he glanced at me again. Tommy?

Tommy, christ, you must mind him – used to work in the building game. Carried the hod or something.

Aw aye, I mind him. Subbied.

You're right, he subbied! Hh! I laughed. That's right man I had forgotten – Tommy, christ: lucky bastard eh! Must've made a real few quid.

McKechnie was watching me. He sniffed and indicated the selection made by one of the racing hacks. According to this cunt Warrior Queen's the only danger.

Aye, I said, it's got a chance. Heh, I wouldnt mind a start subbying somewhere myself, no having to pay any tax or fuck all, eh! that's the way to do it man, know what I mean, if you can get it, that's the way to do it man fuck that tax!

McKechnie was studying the raceform. Hard race but, he said.

I shrugged. Only for second place, favourite's a stonewall, cant get beat.

McKechnie didnt raise his head. Fucking lottery, he muttered.

Another betting show was in progress and I altered my stance a bit, to be able to see the racecard in his newspaper, having to look over his shoulder. When the betting show was over I said: What about yourself man, you working?

Who me? McKechnie sniffed, turned to glance at the screen, rolling up his newspaper at the same time. Hang on a minute, he said, I need a pish.

And he walked off immediately. There was still couple of minutes before the *off*. I went to the nearby wall. The front page of the Sporting Life was tacked here and I browsed the post-mortems on yesterday's results, the jockeys' hard luck stories, all good for a laugh. Then I noticed McKechnie, standing away opposite, beside two old codgers who didnt look to have the price of a packet of Rizlas between them.

I crossed the floor. He had taken a brand new pack of cigarettes from his pocket and was unwrapping the cellophane. He looked at me twice then extended the pack. Ta, I said and had to hold the pack with my left hand while extracting a fag with my right. He stuck the pack back in his pocket. When we were smoking I said: To tell you the truth man I didnt even know you were married never mind in for a divorce!

What! Christ! where've you been? Married – I've been married for years.

Hh!

Years, he said.

Christ! Who to? that wee thing back in Manchester?

He frowned at me. I was well married before I hit that fucking place. He sniffed. She thinks she'll get the wean but she's got no chance.

Good. I nodded. Mind you . . .

Know what I mean, lawyer says I'm a certainty.

Mind you, sometimes . . .

McKechnie said: Hang on a minute, I'm just . . . He turned and squinted up at the formpage on the wall. Then he was edging along to where another punter stood and I could hear him mutter, This Warrior Queen's supposed to have a chance of upsetting the favourite . . .

I stepped over next to him and peered at the form. Could do, I said, but the favourite's got a fair bit of class about her. Won hell of a comfortably last time out and the way I heard it she won hell of a cleverly, a hands and heels game. This is a fucking dawdle man a scoosh case.

The other punter was manoeuvering himself to write out his betting slip in such a way that nobody would see the name of the horse. McKechnie was quiet a moment. Suddenly he thumped the page on the wall. That's the thing I'm feart of, he said, pointing at something.

I looked to see. Dark Lights?

Dark Lights. He nodded, grinned briefly. Dark Lights.

Hh!

Fucking right, he said, know what I think, they've just stuck it in here.

Aw.

Fucking obvious.

I nodded. It has got a chance but you cant always rely on winning form out of maiden races; I mean this is the first time it'll have run in a handicap, and you know yourself that . . .

Hang on a minute. He walked to a different wall where a youth was standing gazing at another formpage. I could see him muttering away.

Then the runners were being loaded into the starting stalls. The youth strode smartly to the counter to place his bet. Shortly afterwards McKechnie had scribbled down his own bet and was striding to the counter, the field now set to come *under starter's orders*. And when the woman had returned him his change and receipt he went to watch the race at the other side of the room altogether.

It was no a bad nightlife in Manchester, I said when I got there. Eh?

What? McKechnie concentrated on the screen.

The nightlife. Manchester. Mind you, it's no bad here if you know where to go. Murder when you're skint but, know what I mean?

He nodded.

Aye, I said.

He sniffed. I've no been here that long.

What? Aw. Christ. Dont worry man dont worry I mean you'll soon find your way about – once you get the hang of their fucking subway system, that tube carry on, up and down and up and down. The buses are good too. And then, when you've got a few quid the gether I mean once you've got a few quid the gether ... I shrugged.

I'm going up the road the morrow.

What?

Aye.

...

He was studying the screen while he spoke, out the corner of his mouth: Edinburgh, I'm going to Edinburgh.

Edinburgh!

Aye.

Christ sake. Edinburgh! I nodded. Mind you, I said, see when ...

Off.

I stopped talking.

The race was over the minimum five furlong trip and soon they were entering the final stretch. Taking the lead at the distance the favourite won going away – exactly the style in which an odds-on shot should win.

A horse by the name of Lucy's Slipper ran on to snatch second place close home. Neither Warrior Queen nor Dark Lights received a mention during the entire race —never showed a leg during the entire race! Typical shite.

But McKechnie was grinning all over his face. Told you, he shouted, I fucking told you!

What? I looked at him.

That favourite, it couldnt get beat, a fucking certainty, I knew it.

Aye, I shrugged. Trained at Epsom as well if you noticed. These Epsom runners usually do good at this track, nice and sharp man, fast as fuck on the firm, hearing the hooves rattle and all that – plus too …

The forecast! McKechnie was chortling and he elbowed me in the ribs: I've dug out the forecast!

What?

The forecast, he said, I've dug it out; that Lucy's Slipper! A certainty for second place! I fucking knew it man I fucking knew it.

Hh.

He winked. I'll tell you something, see the shrewd money? the shrewd money's all down on it. Know what I mean? they've just stuck it in there. Fucking obvious man the forecast. Think they're going to take odds-on for a bet when they can lift five or six to one for a fucking forecast? You kidding! These cunts dont mess about.

Aye, eh.

McKechnie was chortling again. Kept saying it all morning to myself: look for a forecast I says, look for a forecast, this favourite cant get beat, look for a forecast.

McKechnie shook his head, looked at me, then nodded and rubbed at his chin. After a moment he glanced over to the pay-out counter. The youth stood there, holding a receipt in one hand. McKechnie walked across. He was still grinning, then I heard him say: So you got it too?

The youth paused a moment then nodded, then they were comparing notes on the next race in between congratulating each other on the last.

McKechnie copped the next three winners. How did he do it? I thought I was following his trail but I wasnt. I couldnt tell where he was getting his information. Not many guys ever went to the pay-out counter; he was in contact with the couple that did. He kept edging his way in and out of company, eavesdropping here and there. He had this peculiar kind of shuffle, dragging his heels as if his shoes were hell of a heavy – he probably kept a reserve fund stuffed inside his socks the miserable bastard. But I remembered that shuffle and I remembered how he was in Manchester but nothing else about him, except that way he looked at you, he just looked at you ...

I went out for a breath of fresh air. I walked up and down the street a couple of times. Back in the betting shop he kept on the move, especially if I was about. I stepped right in front of him and said: A nicker, just a nicker ...

Aw ... he shrugged.

I'll give you it back man honest, a miserable nicker.

I cant, he said, no the now, I'm sticking the lot on this next favourite. I'll weigh you in after but, dont worry, you'll be alright then – a nicker? aye, no bother, you'll be alright for a nicker.

He about-turned and walked to study a formpage close in beside the two old codgers. The first show of betting came through on the next race. I noticed him watching me, out the corner of his eye. Moments later he did a vanishing act out the door. He probably thinks I didnt see him but I did.

Where I was

At least I am elsewhere. A wind like the soundtrack of a North Pole documentary rages underneath. I have absconded from my former abode leaving neither note nor arrears. I left arrears, I left no cash to discharge them. No explanations of any kind. Simply: I am somewhere else. No persons who knew me then or in fact at any time know of my where-abouts. Season: Midwinter. Equipage: To be listed, but boots as opposed to other things I may have worn previously. And also a leather pouch instead of my old tobacco tin. Jesus, and also a piece of cloth resembling a tartan scarf.

There are no lights. I am resting having walked many miles. I am well wrapped up; brown paper secured round my chest by means of the scarf crossed and tucked inside my trousers, a couple of safety pins are in there somewhere too. My health has got to remain fine otherwise my condition will deteriorate. At present I do not even have a runny nose. I stopped here because of the view. No other reason, none, nothing. I look down between mainland and island. Both masses ending in sheer drops, glowering at each other, but neither quite so high as where I am though maybe they are. Miles separate us. How many, I would be guessing. Rain pours. Sky very grey. The truth is I cannot tell what colour the sky is. May not even be there for all I know. And I reckon it must be past 10 o'clock. A car passed some time ago. A Ford it was but a big one. Expensive model.

Below, the tide reaches up to the head of the loch. No islets visible. My boots are not leaking. I laid out six quid on them. In the glen at the head of the loch are houses; I see lights there, and also opposite where I am a big house can be seen – white during daylight

I imagine. It looks far from safe. Surrounded by tall, bent trees. A cabin cruiser tethered to a narrow jetty. Apart from all this nothing of moment.

Back a distance sheep were nibbling weeds. I saw them from thirty yards and knew what they were immediately.

I left the room in Glasgow recently and got here before the Ford car. There is something good about it all I cannot explain away. Not only the exhilarating gale blowing the dirty skalp clean. Nor the renunciation of all debts relating to the past while. Maybe it is as simple.

From here the road twists and falls to a village where there has to be a pub. As pubs go it shall be averagely not bad. I wont stop. The place will be closed anyway. This afternoon I slept in a public convenience. Clean, rarely used by the smell of it. I should have invested in a tent. Not at all – a good thick waterproof sleepingbag would have been sufficient. I am spending money as I go but have a deal of the stuff, enough to be without worries for some time. If I chance upon a rowing boat tied near the shore I may steal it and visit the island across the way. Unlikely. I could probably swim it. The gap is deceptive but perhaps no more than two miles. Drowning. At one time it would have presented no problem. Never mind.

I enjoy this walking. Amble and race, set off at a trot, and once I ran pell-mell for quite a stretch – until a tractor saw me. Taking baby steps and giant steps, assume odd postures and if a car passes I shriek with laughter. Sing all songs. My jaw aches. My ears ache. Maybe the wind clogs them up.

Noises in my head. Sounding like a lunatic. But my nose remains dry. Probably impending bronchitis. Next time I waken with a bone-dry throat I shall know for sure. When I become immune to the wind everything will be fine. Immune to the wind.

Well stocked up on tobacco, always carrying cheese and whisky in case of emergencies; fever and that. The notion of buying a pipe. I have no room for useless piles of tobacco. I handrolled pipe tobacco in the past. Terrible stuff.

From Arivruach the road curves steeply through a glen owned by someone whose name escapes me. Stiff climb. Tired my knees in particular. For the eventual relief of walking with straight legs I firstly walked with bent ones, at the knees. Black specks in front or slightly above my eyes. The blood cannot be as good as the best. But the wind, I heard it all the time. Loud racket never dying. I thought of climbing a mountain. The real problem is rain. Whenever it falls I am affected. Soaks in knocking my hearing out. I am unable to look up for any length of time. It is damaging my boots and perhaps my coat. If my hair is plastered down over my brow in too irritating a manner water will drip down my sleeve when I push it up. Terrible sensation. The vehicles splash me. The face red raw; my nose must be purple, the constant drip drip from either nostril. Beads hang onto my eyebrows, cling at my eyelashes, falling from my chin down my neck – from the hair at my back down my neck it streams down my spinal cord, gets rubbed and rubbed by my trouser waistband into the skin at the small of my back. And no respite for my hands inside the coat pockets. The sleeves of this coat are far too wide so only my flesh actually enters each pocket, the wet cloth irritating my wrists, and tiny pools of water gathering within the nylon material. The rain spoils the walk but it brightens. Always brightens eventually. Then I see water on the leaves of bushes and I can skite the branch of a tree to see beads drop. The road dries in patches, swiftly, sometimes I can sit on such a spot though not for long of course.

In the future I hope to sleep during the day, regularly. Apparently some people do sleep on their feet the bastards. And I try striding with my eyes shut once I have noted the direction.

I enjoy night. Not dusk so much because I know pubs do business; possibly it gets easier once the days lengthen. I shall sleep all day perhaps. With this constant exercise four hours' kip wont be enough. And I shall be swimming when the water heats. Eating does not worry me yet. My money will run out. My best sleep so far was had in a hostel closed for the winter. Very simple to enter. No food but plenty of firewood which burned fine. I spread all my clothes on the backs of chairs in front of it. And washed both pairs of socks. And had a complete bodywash which might not have been a good idea since two or three layers of old skin went down the drain. This explains why I am freezing. Unfortunately I appear to be really particular about clean feet thus socks although I do not bother about underwear, seldom have any. Up until the wash I was wearing each pair on alternate days and both when sleeping. They had a stale, damp smell. My feet were never wholly dry. Small particles stuck to the toejoints, the soles. I had to see all this during the socks-changing process. In future I may steel myself if warmer feet can be guaranteed. And may even take to wearing both pairs daily, in other words keep them on at all times. Christ I wont be surprised if I catch the flu. I have acted very foolishly. No wonder tramps wash rarely. Yet what happens when the summer comes and I want a swim.

I considered staying in the hostel indefinitely. I could also have erected a sign for other wayfarers explaining how easy it was to break and enter, but did not. The reason reflects badly on me.

This day was bitter. Never warm inside the coat. That fucking wind went through me. Tried everything from walking sideways to hiding behind trees. All I could finally do was stride along punching my boots hard down on the road with my shoulders rigid, hunched up. This induced prolonged shivering but was the best I could manage. Every part of me cold, sick cold. Now and then I stopped for a swig of the stuff.

When the road closed onto the water again I cut off through the marsh and down to the edge of the loch or maybe it was the sea. There was land far out. An island? Amazing silence. Nothing but the waves breaking, lapping in over the pebbles. Where I was the wind was forgotten. Almost warm. I took off the coat and used it as a cushion on a dry rock a little way back. No fishing boats. I saw only small birds, landbirds, the country equivalent to sparrows I suppose. My mind got into a certain state. The usual blankness. A trance or something like it. Time obviously passed. Clear, a clarity. I finished my whisky and chain-smoked. Staying put. No wish to walk the shore in search of a better position. The rain came later. Fine drizzle, spotting the water. I watched on for a bit then had to put the coat across my shoulders and shelter beneath the trees. But I remained for quite a while and might have pitched a tent there.

Extra cup

I was to wait in the waiting room, somebody would come to collect me. To pass the time I thumbed through the stack of industrial magazines, eventually dozing off until the door banged open. It was a clerk, clutching a sheaf of fulscapaper, he frowned and told me to follow him; he led me out the gatehouse, through the massive carpark and into a side entrance, along a corridor between offices then out, and across waste ground into another building where I followed him along the side of a vast machineroom into a long tunnel and out through rubber swing doors, onto more waste ground but now with rail tracks crossing here and there, and into another building via a short tunnel leading sharply down then up a concrete incline at the top of which we entered an ancient hoist with criss-cross iron gates to go clanking downwards to a subfloor where the clerk questioned a youth on the whereabouts of a Mr Lambton, but received only a shrug in reply; on we went along a corridor, a deep thumping sound coming to the right of us and men occasionally appearing out of doorways and entering others, pushing all manner of trolleys, bogeys and barrows, and we followed one of them outside and across more waste ground, bypassing one building and into another where we found Mr Lambton sitting on an upturned crate behind a big machine. He saw us but continued chatting to a dungareed man perched on a sort of balcony near the top of the machine, a rag covering his head he looked to be greasing the moving parts which were of course stationary at present. Then Mr Lambton ground out the cigarette he had been smoking and turned to say: What's up with you Eric? Something worrying you is there?

It's the new sweeperup, George.

New sweeperup?

The clerk sighed.

Mr Lambton laughed and winked up at the man on the machine then he glanced at me and nodded, and the clerk strode off. After a moment he continued chatting to the man on the machine. The man on the machine nodded now and again but never spoke. Eventually Mr Lambton said to me, You know the lay-out of this Block?

No.

I'll show you then eh! He smiled and got up from the crate; he yawned and stretched, and sighed before setting off. Every so often he would pause and indicate a machine, maybe telling me what it did in relation to a different machine. He led me outside and we walked round the building and he showed me the railway tracks and pointed out other buildings, occasionally denoting them by number. He knew a great many people and stopped to talk fairly often. Soon a bell was ringing. And I realised we were back where we had started, behind the big machine. Mr Lambton chuckled when he noticed me noticing this and he walked on. He opened a door and I followed him through rows and rows of wall-to-ceiling racks. We came upon a dozen men sitting either on upturned boxes or sacking on the floor; it was teabreak. An elderly man was pouring from a big urn. Mr Lambton called: Extra cup Bert.

Bert didnt answer.

Cup, extra cup – new man Bert, new man.

Bert glanced along at Mr Lambton and grumbled unintelligibly, continued pouring tea then passed the cups out one by one to the nearest seated men who then passed them along to the others.

Alright? called Mr Lambton. And when he received no reply he grinned at me, raised his eyebrows and walked back the way we had come.

The elderly man didnt give me out a cup of tea but he glanced at me as though I should understand there were no extra ones to be had. Soon the bell was ringing and the men rising and leaving. Bert didnt move; he was sitting near the urn, still munching a sandwich, gazing at the foot of the racks facing him. I got up and walked along and poured myself the last of the tea into one of the assorted cups left by the men. Bert noticed and grumbled.

Did you want it? I said.

He didnt reply; he reached for a newspaper left by the men and unfolded it, brought a spectacle case out from the top pocket of his dungarees, and began reading. Then he looked up: Sweeperup are you? You're supposed to help me you know. Dont suppose he told you that though eh! Did he?

Aye, but he said you'd tell me the score.

Hh! Bert shook his head and returned his attention to the newspaper. A few minutes later he put the spectacles back in the case and snapped it shut, put away the newspaper and got onto his feet. He began collecting in the empty cups and the discarded sandwich wrappings. I helped him. There was a brush leaning against a rack; I brushed the floor.

Leave that, he said. He waved me to come with him. We walked through the rows of racks in a direction different to the one used by the men to exit, and arrived at a small door which had two sections, the bottom and top halves being separate. Bert unsnibbed the bottom half and opened it very quietly, he peered out to the left and to the right, then motioned me to follow him across the corridor and into another room; once inside he cut off to the corner and I followed him there, and up a short flight of stairs. When he looked at me I saw the corner of his mouth twitching, then he frowned and opened a door. It was a tiny room with lockers and a long bench. He sighed and withdrew another newspaper from a pocket inside his dungarees and sat down, and took out his spectacle case; flapping the newspaper open he sighed again, began reading. About twenty minutes passed. He got up and walked to the wall to his left and moved a calendar; there was a peephole, he looked through it. Then we went all the way back again and he collected two brushes, giving me one. Come on, he said. He led me around the building for a time then as we turned a corner the clerk appeared from along a corridor. He came striding towards us, gesticulating at me. You've to come to the office, he cried, Mrs Willmott wants a word.

I turned to Bert but he wasnt there. And the clerk was striding off down the corridor. I went quickly after him, out through the rubber doors and across the waste ground, and so on eventually into a building which seemed to consist solely of offices, and I followed him into one with Mrs Willmott's name on the door. She was a young woman, sitting at a wide desk. The clerk closed the door behind me and she glanced upwards, but continued studying a sheet of fulscapaper then reached to a filing cabinet to take out another one, and after a bit she said, New sweeperup … Do you have your things? your card and so forth.

No, sorry.

You dont?

No, sorry.

O for heaven sake.

I'm really sorry. I laid them out on the table last night all set for this morning but then I forgot to lift them because I was late and having to rush for the bus, it's because I'm

Well you must bring them tomorrow you know there is no excuse; if you dont you'll simply be obliged to return home for them.

Fine, I'll make sure, definitely. What I'll do, I'll stick them right into my pocket as soon as I get home.

A buzzer sounded. The door opened and in came the clerk, and he carried straight on out again so that I was to follow him. On this occasion he left me at the ancient hoist. I returned to the building where he had led me earlier. The machines were being run-down. Sure enough it was dinner-break. In the washroom the men were washing their hands and their wrists and crumpling the used paper towels into an empty crate. I walked along the corridor and into the room with the wall-to-ceiling racks, just as the bell started ringing. Bert was spreading out the cups on the upturned crate he used as a table. The men began arriving and taking their seats, opening their parcels of sandwiches and laying their newspapers out on their laps. Bert indicated a cup lying a little apart from the rest; it was for me. There was an old newspaper in the empty crate they used for rubbish. I sat reading this for a while. My belly began rumbling and the man sitting next to me loudly flourished his newspaper while turning the next page. Is there a canteen? I said.

He frowned. A man further along from him called: Canteen? course there's a canteen. Eh Reg! he called to another man. The canteen now where is that? Group 3?

Group 2, 6 Block.

On the other side of me Bert snorted and he leaned over to spit into the empty crate. Some of the men watched him. The one named Reg frowned. Yeah, he said, Group 2, 6 Block.

There was a short silence. Bert gazed at the rack opposite where he sat, and he said: Group 5 it is, if it's the canteen you're talking about.

Bert's right, nodded another man, it's got to be nearer 5 than 3.

Got to be nearer 5 than 3 … Reg stared at him. What d'you mean it's got to be nearer, why the bleeding hell's it got to be nearer?

It was Bert replied. Cause when they bleeding changed it Reg that's why.

Reg shook his head.

You sure? said somebody but Bert didnt answer. He was munching a sandwich. He stopped at the crusts and tossed them into the rubbish crate, he glanced along at Reg and sighed. Then someone else began discussing the old canteen in relation to the new one and another joined in by relating this to why the new canteen had had to be built from scratch more or less, instead of just simply refurbishing the old one. A man got up and strolled along the row, pausing to read slips of paper sticking out from the articles stored on the racks. Bert nudged me and gestured at a newspaper lying on the floor and I handed it to him. Most of the other men were now leaving, as though going for a walk down the corridor to pass the time. When the bell did ring I lifted the brush to begin sweeping the place but I was finding a great deal of dust lying on the articles along the bottom racks and so I got an old rag and used it to give them a wipe down first. Bert looked in without saying anything, and went away again. Mr Lambton appeared later and he chatted with me for a bit on general matters to do with the building we were in, finally telling me to continue sweeping in the machineroom. I nodded. Once he had gone I carried on dusting the articles at the foot of the racks for a while, before leaving. I took the brush with me. Going along the corridor I caught a glimpse of Bert through in the machineroom, brushing between two big machines. He waved me in. I nodded and continued along the corridor and straight out, across the waste ground and into the next building, and so on until eventually I was in the one with the offices.

It's not the job for me, I said to Mrs Willmott.

I see. She nodded. You havent given it much of a chance.

I just eh – well, I think it's best to make the decision now rather than hang on hoping I'll get used to it.

She shook her head. I wont attempt to dissuade you Mr aaaa … She reached for the sheet of fulscapaper from the filing cabinet and paused; she glanced at me: You didnt bring your things this morning?

No, I left them – remember? I was to bring them tomorrow morning.

Mm … She closed the drawer and shifted on her chair. She looked at me, before studying the sheet of fulscapaper, and lifting a pen. Is this your address? she said while settling to begin copying it down on another sheet.

Yes but I'll be leaving it.

O.

If you were going to send me anything.

Well, she shrugged, the money.

Could you not just give me it the now?

Mm.

I'll probably be leaving tonight, or early tomorrow morning, so … She clicked her tongue on her top teeth then sighed, picked up the receiver of her internal telephone and asked a Miss Arnold to come in please. When Miss Anold arrived she got up from her chair and they both went out into the corridor, shutting the door behind them.

About ten minutes passed. There were calendars and framed certificates on the wall.

Mrs Willmott returned alone, she laid a day's wages on her desk and put forwards a receipt for me to sign. I did so, lifted the money and slid it into my left front trouser pocket. She sniffed and went to the door, opened it for me. Thanks, I said, taking the brush from where I had parked it against the wall.

I had to return to the building where I had been working to collect my jerkin. Bert wasnt about. I laid the brush near to the upturned crate he used for the rubbish then I left immediately.

learning the Story

I once met an old lady sitting under a bridge over the River Kelvin. She smoked Capstan full-strength cigarettes and played the mouthorgan.

The moon was well up as I had passed along the footpath listening to the water fall at the small dam beyond the old mill. Aye, cried the voice, you are there are you! If I had spotted her before she had me I would have crept back the way I had come. Aye, she cried again. And rising to her feet she brought out the mouthorgan from somewhere inside the layers of her clothing, and struck up the tune: Maxwelton Braes Are Bonny was the name of it. Halfway through she suddenly stopped and she stared at me and grunted something. She sat down again on the damp grass with her back against the wall at the tunnel entrance; she stared at her boots. Very good that, I said to her. From her shopping bag she pulled out the packet of Capstan full-strength cigarettes. She sniffed. And I felt as if I had let her down. I always liked that tune, I told her. She struck a match and lighted a cigarette. She flicked the match a distance and it landed with smoke still rising from it. Drawing the shopping bag in between her raised knees she inhaled deeply, exhaled staring at her boots. Cheerio then, I said. I paced on beneath the bridge aware of my footsteps echoing.

The old lady wore specs and had a scarf wrapped round her neck. Her nose was bony. Her skirt may have showed under the hem of her coat. When she was playing the mouthorgan she had moved slightly from foot to foot. Her coat was furry.

Getting there

I stayed with the lorry and bypassed the dump. Down the A74 the driver was turning off into the weird Leadhills so I got out. I remained on this side of the road. A van. The driver wasnt going far, not beyond Lockerbie. I went. I spotted an inn in the distance and told him to stop, I felt like a couple of pints. Four customers including myself. Moving to a table within earshot I tried to concentrate on what they were saying but difficult to make heads or tails of, not just the accents.

I still had money. I had enough to rent some accomodation in the inn for the night and get rid of the beard and the grime and the old skin before returning down the road.

The man refused me a room. Full up. I was really surprised. I had expected a refusal of course but at the same time hadnt. He said the rooms were all taken. Aye. May his teeth fall out and his hair recede the bastard, saying the rooms were all taken yet allowing me to stay drinking his beer. I was being sociable, a bit sorry for them, not wanting to hurt their feelings by exiting too early for christ sake.

Enough. I had to vanish in England. And I didnt have to fucking walk either, I had enough for a fucking bus. Or a train maybe. But the lift came almost at once and soon I was crossing the border.

The Appleton Arms. Pint of bitter and a pastie with mustard. A husband and wife behind the bar: no bother the bed and breakfast sir. One could only sigh. The outside lavatory with an ancient bicycle parked against the washbasin. Upstairs to immerse for twenty minutes in the grime and old skin then out for a smooth shave, and then back into the bath again till finally emerging in the pink. The desire for newly suiting, never seen nor heard of outside of books by bad authors; the freshly-pressed linen underwear and silk pyjamas, the valet to disrobe one, the smoking jacket velvet Jobson yes, hock shall do ably with the old cheese & water biscuits and fly invitations to the chambermaid.

The bed was soft, sagging in the centre, but I slept amazing and woke in fine fettle, in plenty of time for breakfast which was sadly meagre but good cups of dark red tea with plenty of toast to atone.

Waiting halfway up the slip road onto the M6 I allowed three lifts to go by, attempting to explain that it had to be London or bust. Springtime in old King's Cross. But I could see the drivers' faces tightening into huffs at the perceived rejection. I feel bad about that; three probables vanishing from the paths of other wayfarers.

Then the rain of course.

So aye – Bristol? Aye, yes, Bristol, Bristol's fine mate. Maybe the M4 or something.

Very snug inside the big artic, the driver's music blasting it out and no need to gab but just enjoy the ride down the safe inside lane, the drone of the windscreen-wipers while the rain, battering hard down on the cabin roof. Fuck the M4.

I liked Bristol on sight. Something about the place. Yet I couldnt remember passing through it before. As though last time along I maybe missed it. But I had been heading northwest, detouring via Wales and according to maps the passing through Bristol is inevitable. That is a strange thing.

Windswept Weymouth and nothing to add except I still had money.

A bad time aboard. Pounding waves. Passengers having to heave out their guts here there and everywhere; the mess on the saloon foor, it streaming about, the bits of meat and veg amongst the Guinness-type froth but the grumpy barman stood me a pint when he saw I wasnt getting affected. I told him a yarn about working on the boats off Cromarty – in fact it must have been down to the time spent plying Glasgow buses over cobbled streets, those bone-shaking old efforts probably ensuring I can never be seasick again. And so pleased with myself I might have ordered a three-course meal if the cash had stretched.

…

An old guy had been tethering a group of rowing boats, down on the beach, to the side of a wee pier; then he sat on a deck chair up by a green hut which was advertising fishing tackle for hire. Going over to him and saying: I want your job ya old bastard.

…

This island. And so long it took to accept the warmer weather as a fact. It bringing out a great many people, all young-looking for some reason maybe to do with the summer looming ahead. The jeans and T-shirts and sandals. Even on the concrete promenade my feet are comfortable.

The clouds are not in sight.

In a delicatessen I could buy 2 ounces of cold spiced sausage and rolls. Narrow streets and pavements and all of the tiny shops. The promenade is very long and straight. Word of an old castle. The rest of it to be explored. In a pub later on I was sitting at the bar eavesdropping on the chat of three girls who were sipping at blackcurrant & Pernod

and the sensation of being offered the opportunity, I could have explained the present predicament

but there was nothing to be said then till finally it was too too late, too late, it getting dark, and the rain drizzling, drizzling.

Staying there in the bar, my back to a partition wall – yet still content – the feet outstretched beneath the table and tucking them under when someone walked by, with apologies articulated that I might reasonably be understood. Clearing the accent to please, in other words; in a good way but.

The barmaid roused me. It was around half past midnight.

I knew all about the police hereabouts. Throw you off the place at the slightest excuse – unfixed abodes the especial cause. Twice in ten minutes I had to go down an alley to piss. Yet I still wasnt too worried, it was so very dark, so very quiet, and neither strollers nor stray animals. A patrol car rolled by. I had the smoke cupped in the palm of my right hand.

Now the rain.

Out onto the promenade I cut smartly across, down the stone steps to the sands immediately below the big stone wall; fast along to the farthest point and up, retracking to the third last shelter. I had to take this chance I think though well aware it was obvious, unsafe. I sat on the bench in the side exposed to the Sea, elbows on knees and hands propping up the head. The rain belting down, like a storm, the incredible noise. I was probably trying to sort out certain things about the dump and being here instead of there but I dont remember doing any of that at all, just entering a kind of daze, a kind of numbness, literally, having to get up and hop about to regain sensation proper. And the rain blowing in, having to huddle into the side of the wall, escaping the wind but the draughts, the draughts were just not, they were too much – not too much, just, they were just, they were like the wind, sudden blasts. And this strange experience of hearing a clock strike. I had no idea of time, I had sixteen pence in my pocket. Then later, later on, through the blackest greys a little bit of red showed in snatches; enough for the luck to be hitting on. I knew it. A certainty. No need to hop.

...

The tide was out. I walked the sands a furlong or so, the boots squeaking then squelching. Sand worms. Red veins. So so tiny, thin. The first time I ever saw them though I had often looked at the mound of twirls they left dotted about. Amazing. What are they like at all, the red things. And sitting on my heels gazing back to the promenade, the row of villas, guest-houses and hotels. And back at the Sea, two boats an inch apart on the horizon.

the paperbag

What was the point anyway, there didnt seem to be any at all. I footered about with the newspaper, no longer even pretending interest. It was useless. I felt totally useless – I was useless, totally. I crumpled the newspaper in both hands, watching it, seeing the shapes it made, the way its pages became.

I would go on a walk; that was what to do. I uncrumpled the newspaper and rolled it into a neat sort of bundle, to carry it in my right hand, and then began walking. O christ but it was good to be alive – really. Really and truly. I felt magnificent. Absolutely wonderful. What was it about this life that made a body feel so good, so absolutely fucking wonderful. Was everybody the same. Now I was chuckling. Not too loudly but, no point worrying folk. A woman approached, her message bags not too full, preoccupied, the slight smile on her face. Where else could it be? Her eyes. Her eyes could be smiling. Is that possible? I was chuckling again. And then the mongrel appeared. I recognized it right away: a stupid kind of beast, even how it trotted was a bit stupid – plus that something about it, that odd look it could give – as though it was a fucking mule! Mule. Why did I think of that, mule. Well it was a beast and it was stupid-looking – or rather, it behaved stupidly, the way it looked at folk and didnt do as they desired, they wanted it off the pavement out their road, it just carried on trotting till sometimes they even had to get out of its road. Amazing. Imagine giving it a kick! Just going up and giving it a kick. Or else poisoning it. Taking it away on a long walk and then dumping it. Maybe on a bus journey right out the other side of the city, pushing it off and shutting the door, leaving the thing yelping in astonishment. What will happen to me now! Christ sake the dirty bastard he's pushed me off the bus and shut the door and I dont know where I've landed!

Imagine being a dog but – murder! people taking you wherever they like and you dont have a say in the matter. Here boy, here boy. I would hate to be a dog like that, getting ordered about by cunts without knowing what for, not having a genuine say on the matter. Horrible, really fucking horrible. And then getting put down for christ sake sometimes for nothing, no reason, just for doing what dogs do. Biting people!

Crazy, walking along the road thinking about such stuff. Absolute fucking nonsense. Mongrels by christ! But that is what happens. And thinking of that is better than thinking of nothing. I would say so anyway. Or would I? The trouble with being useless is this thinking; it becomes routine, you cannot stop yourself. I think all the time, even when I'm reading my newspaper. And the things I think about are fucking crazy. Imagine going up to somebody and saying Hey, have you ever felt like screwing the queen? Just to actually say it to somebody. Incredible. This is the kind of thing I can think about. I cannot help it. I didnt always think like it either. I used to think about ordinary things. Or did I? I find it hard to tell.

Then she was coming towards me but I didnt notice properly until there we were having to get out each other's road. Sorry, I said and I smiled in a hopeful manner. I was lost in abstraction …

And then I smiled coyly, this coyliness compensating for the use of the long word, abstraction. But everything was fine, everything was fine, she understood. It's okay, she replied, I was a bit abstracted myself.

And of course she was! Otherwise she would have fucking bumped into me if she hadnt been careful to get out my road while I was getting out of hers!

Then she had dropped a paperbag and was bending down to retrieve it; and once she had retrieved it she opened it and peered inside.

And so did I!

I just fucking stretched forwards and poked my head next to hers. Not in any sort of ambiguous way, just to peer into the bag same as her. She glanced at me, quite surprised. Then we smiled at each other as though in appreciation of the absurdity of my reaction. And yet it had been a true reaction. Normally I'm not a nosey person. But having said all of that I have to confess that it maybe was a bit ambiguous, maybe I was trying to get a bit closer to her because it should be said that she was nice, in fact she was really nice. The way she was standing there and then bending to get her paperbag etc., the smile she had, and above all that understanding, how she had eh o christ o christ, o christ and there wasnt anything I could say, nothing, nothing at all because I was without funds, absolutely fucking without funds. So after a wee moment I smiled, an unhealthy smile – even at the actual instant it was happening I was thinking how it would be to have a blunderbuss whose muzzle I could stick my head into and then pull the trigger.

It was a surprise to see her still standing there. How come she was still standing there the way things were. I didnt even know her. I had never seen her before in all my life. I said: Eh d'you live roundabout?

But she didnt reply. She was frowning at something. She hadnt paid the slightest attention to what I said. And no wonder, the things I say, they are always so fucking boring, so fucking boring. Why am I the most fucking boring bastard in the whole fucking world? Her cake was bashed. Inside her paperbag was a cake and it had become bashed because of falling on the pavement. I could have mentioned that to her. That was something to say, instead of this, this fucking standing, just fucking standing there, almost greeting, greeting my eyes out. I was just standing there having to stop myself greeting like a wean, looking at her, trying to make her see and by making her see stopping msyelf and making everything fine, if she would just stay on a minute or two and we could maybe have a chat or something – just a couple of minutes' chat, that would have worked the oracle, maybe, to let her see. Because after all, she hadnt been put off by the way I had peered into her paperbag. She had recognized it as a plain ordinary reaction, the sort of thing that happens out of curiosity – a bit stupid right enough; the way a kid acts. And yet she hadnt been put off. Not even as a person had I put her off. She smiled at me, a true smile – there again, it had happened at the point of departure

for yes, that moment had indeed arrived and was gone now, gone forever. And so too was she, trotting along the pavement, away to a life that was much better than this one. If I could run after her and clasp her by the hand.

I had unrolled the newspaper and was glancing at the back page, an item of football news. I could just have run after her and said Sorry for having almost bumped right into her and making her drop the paperbag. But what was the point of it all? it was useless, totally fucking useless. I crumpled the newspaper in my right hand then grabbed it from there with my left, and continued the walk.

Old Holborn

He was pounding away on the guitar and mouthorgan as if it was 1968. A sad sight during this overcast morning in central December. I had been coming along the pavement, caught a glimpse of something just off the kerb – silver paper, poking out from under a half brick. Then this music. Dear god. He paused to take a tobacco pouch out from his jacket pocket. Bad time of year for this game, I said, eh? this weather! fucking murder.

He didnt say anything, he spread the tobacco along the rice paper.

Carols, I said, it's carols you should be giving them. This time of year man that's what they're fucking looking for, carols.

Could be right jock, he said.

Jesus christ the accent! What a relief hearing a London voice man where you from?

London's right.

Well well well, London eh! Heh what's that? I sniffed. Old Holborn a mile …

Yeh jock. He licked the gummed edge and handed me the pouch while bringing out a box of matches.

I rolled one quickly then said: How long you been here?

Half an hour.

I nodded. He handed me the box of matches. When I inhaled I went into a fit of coughing, it ended in a bout of the sneezes. Always the same. I gave my nose a wipe. That first drag man, it's always the same. Nectar but. Bad for you as well, so they say. Hh – makes you think right enough.

He was looking along the road. An old tobacco tin was lying to the side, by his feet. I nudged it with the toe of my left shoe; about thirty two pence maybe. Christ sake, half an hour too!

Yeh, bleeding hopeless jock. He began to footer with the musical instruments and then launched into a dirge of some kind. No wonder he was skint. Not a bad guitarist but the song he sang was rotten and he couldnt sing very good. The pedestrians marched past. I lifted the tobacco tin. He looked at me.

It's alright man, I'll do your collecting.

He didnt answer, continued the singing. A middle-aged man with a rolled up brolly approaching.

Couple of bob for the singer jimmy couple of bob for the singer! Eh? I stood in front of him, holding the tin beneath his chin and into it he dropped a ten-pence piece. Easy business. Next along came a man and woman. Heh jimmy, I said, the singer, what about the singer? Eh missis? a couple of bob for the singer?

The purse snapped open and she dropped in some copper stuff while he chipped in with another ten-pence piece. The next miserable bastard carried on marching, his ears purpling when I shouted after him. In this game you can get so you want to strangle some cunt; it's best not taking it personally. Savage glares and leave it at that. Once or twice I was having to catch myself up from chasing some of them. While your man there continued with the singing. Young boys and lassies were the best; they thought it a good laugh, maybe because of the accent. But they usually came across and the tobacco tin soon was rattling in the healthy manner. Then he stopped; the singing had been deteriorating anyway. He brought out the pouch, rolled himself a smoke. He said: Can you sing jock?

No me man I'm no up on that country and western stuff – Dell Shannon I'm into.

Folkrock, he said, frowning. I dont sing that country crap.

Aw.

Dell Shannon … he nodded.

I always forget the bastarn words but. I've been trying to sing that *Runaway* for years man.

He shrugged, glanced across the road: a post office with a big clock in the window. He started strumming the guitar in an absent-minded way. I cleared my throat and began to sing, and he stopped strumming immediately. Fucking hell, he muttered.

Naw, I said, I usually just remember the words when I hear the thing getting sung. Heh what about *Kelly*? D'you know that *Kelly* at all?

He scratched at his ear, glanced at the tobacco tin on the ground, then up and down the street, before shifting the glance into my direction, but without really looking at me. What about Dylan, he said, you got to know some Dylan?

Dylan … aw aye, Dylan …

He was looking at me now.

Course, I said.

Right then jock. On you go. I'll pick it out … He sniffed watching a well-dressed woman walk by. He sniffed again. Alright?

Aye, fine. And I began straight in on that one *The Hard Rain Is Gonna Fall* but I tailed off long before entering the second verse. I tried to keep it going by repeating the opening one. He kept on with the strumming but without hardly blowing the mouthorgan. Fucking hopeless. No point. People were just walking past too. I stopped singing. Look, I said, we were doing good with me just collecting. Know what I mean? Better off sticking to that. You do the singing and I'll hold the tin. At least we'll get a fucking wage out it!

He shook his head.

How no?

He shrugged, started picking away on the individual guitar strings and it was making a tune. It sounded fine.

You just do that, I said.

No good jock, they dont want to know.

Well at least give it a try man I mean if you're

How much I got in the tin?

Nearly two quid – heh, fancy a pie and a pint?

Just had me breakfast jock.

Breakfast!

Yeh.

Hh.

He turned away and gave a sharp rasp on the mouthorgan and launched into another fucking dirge.

Tell you something, I said, I've no eaten for days – days! A tin of fucking sardines man! And you talk about breakfast! Breakfast by fuck.

He nodded, still involved in the music. I grabbed the tin up from the pavement. He stopped playing and shook his head at me. I put the tin back down. He continued playing.

What's up? I said.

He didnt reply.

Heh man what's up?

He paused to say, Leave it out jock.

Leave what fucking out, you'd still have thirty fucking pee if it wasnt for me.

Yeh, he said, yeh, that's the fucking problem mate too heavy, ten more minutes of you and the man would be here sticking me for extortion.

What?

Yeh.

What did you say?

You heard.

I nodded. Right, I said, well I'll tell you something for nothing. I'm due a couple of bob off you … I reached to nudge the tobacco tin with my left toe again. Then I bent quickly and lifted it. At least fifty pence, I said, I'm due fifty pence.

Take a pound.

Fifty's plenty.

Take the bleeding pound jock for christ sake.

Okay then. I'm really starving man honest. Heh, listen, you want me to get you something? A half ounce of Old Holborn? I mean … I shrugged. Whatever. If you want something …

I got enough.

Pint of milk maybe?

He shook his head. He continued with his singing.

Okay then, I said, ta. I'll be back shortly.

I didnt go back of course – doubtful whether he would have been there anyway.

O jesus, here come the dwarfs

When the dwarfs appear everything is at an end. All you ever fixed. The lot. All gone. On the Thursday night they are there. The process of rapid disintegration then follows. Until that point problems do not exist. Problems? what are they at all! no such things. Afterwards there is nothing else.

Dwarfs never have anything fixed, plans have not been laid down, there are no 'eventualities'. They have nothing whatsoever. Yet they come and they take over. And they look at each other as though joined at the nose, while the feet are being cawed from the very ground you walk upon. Nothing can remain the same. Tents will have started collapsing. Those previously occupied are mysteriously void. Dustbins have been overspilling their contents into the long grass. Television sets explode without causal explanation. And the swimming pool is become infested by insects and wee dods of animal shite. Moles. Moles are burrowing beneath groundsheets apparently. All the things, they all stop working. Continual reports of blocked toilet bowls and sinks; and a pile of pots has been found behind the kitchen area. These pots used to be fine but are now food-encrusted beyond repair; and the smells, all the smells, now encroaching throughout the walking area. And into this same walking area come farm animals, bleating. And the site-shop seems to have ceased trading: the wee woman from the village no longer arrives first thing in the morning – that great wee woman who always gave you the cheery nod and allowed you the couple of grocery items plus tobacco on tick till wagesday no problem if the coast was clear.

All gone. All of it.

Yet though holidaymakers may grumble the dwarfs will remain silent. Dwarfs dont grumble. They just smile, are humble, are thoughtful to others. They go dashing around endeavouring to help, ostensibly existing for your especial convenience whereas the reality: you are being set fair for a corner wherein the possibility of laying down your life is advancing. Do not believe in their smile. It is not happy-go-lucky. They have arrived in the pub on Thursday evening because tomorrow you get your wages. When first you bear witness to 'the voice' your puzzled but immediate response is to fuck off home to the tent. This you will not do, having some vague notion that by remaining aloof you must influence events; thus you stand there, awaiting the barman, gradually becoming aware that a cloud of staggering proportions has settled above your head. It is all over. Chance could have reaped a future as secure as this. Aye, of course your defences were down. A Thursday evening. You are tired out, only just managing to tap Pierre for the price of a couple of beers, enough to see you through the evening in a quiet way. What energy you had got you thus far and no more.

With determined nonchalance you will carry your pint to the domino table to sit on the fringe of the onlookers. But the nodded greeting to such as Emil or Jaques was perfunctory, you are pre-occupied by something, unable to grasp quite what it is. Then 'the voice', again disrupting, disruptive, your very thoughts, your single most personal and solitary thoughts. Then you are amazed to realize that some sort of inflexion of the voices from the bar was giving you to understand that you were supposed to be charging across the room crying Welcome dwarfs welcome! It is incredible. You lean forwards, place your pint on the ledge beneath the table, rest your elbows on your knees, attempting to devote your complete attention to the game of dominoes. But this is not the weekend, it is Thursday evening and the bar is not full to bursting with exuberant holidaymakers. Voices echo. The dwarfs know fine well you can hear them. It is what they intend. Their voices can and must be heard. At this stage you are not quite admitting your quandry and are willing to indulge in such internal asides as: Am I hearing things! hoping against hope that the consequent ironic smile about your mouth will be noticed. But so what if it is? And why are you in this position in the first place? Is there anybody there to answer such questions? How come you are having to ask them? What the fuck is it? What is going on? Maybe you are hearing things after all. Thursday night, you've been tired out, too knackered to cook yourself a meal, you just washed and came straight down the pub; maybe you're fucking hallucinating. No matter, for by this time you are unable to contain the pressure – your belly, it has been churning – the beer giving you heartburn, the tobacco maybe, burning your lips and causing that dryness in the mouth and you're having to tighten your lips and close your eyelids, trying to suppress the rage. It is rage; you are raging, you have lifted your pint but your hand is shaking and you slam the pint glass down onto the table and jump to your feet and go marching across to deliver the most bitter diatribe ever heard in the pub. But the dwarfs are just sitting there, occasionally drawing their noses together. Are they naive? Is that all it is? How can you tell? You cannot tell. There is no surefire way of knowing. And you are sitting at their table. Here you are on a chair adjacent to theirs. And the questions are coming at you from all angles and if you dont put a stop to it immediately you are seconds away from giving a moment by moment account of all, all the things. Those pauses occurring in the conversation. Aye, you were about to speak. You must be alert, you have to sit there saying nothing, turning pauses into longer pauses. Or questions into questions: you can turn questions into questions. Tax them on their existence, on their experience, their expectations – above all else their expectations. What precisely is it they are demanding of you? What is it that you are to be having done? Well for starters: consider the things you never classed as problems because of your studied attention to possible eventualities – the things you classified under the banner 'impossible'. Not only have the dwarfs encountered such problems, they have surmounted them. Apparently without having realized it. They havent even realized those things were problems, they just fucking went ahead and got beyond them. And they are gaping at you, at your irritation. They have no comprehension as to its cause, and will look to each other as though joined at the nose. Meanwhile you do not feel a mug. Somehow you are given to understand that you yourself are the one individual present who genuinely is aware of the central ins and outs. Only you know the truth, that you are a fucking mug, that you have never known anything, nothing, nothing whatsoever. It is odd, You will sit for a moment, gazing into space, then jump up and rush to the domino table to collect your pint and your tobacco and matches, and back with the dwarfs you … Back with the dwarfs? Aye, exactly, of your own volition, you have returned to their table. It really is fucking incredible. You will look at them for signs of guilt but why should there be? Do they have cause for guilt? It was you returned to sit beside them. You stare at them, and discover that the pint you are holding contains a fresh quantity of beer; it's not the same pint at all; you swallowed the remains of the first in a gulp and the dwarfs have bought you a second. There is no deceit. Everything is out in the open and being accomplished fairly. They are actually insisting that they dont want a drink in return. They dont want one. They maybe know you are skint because it's a Thursday evening and are quite rightly opposed to you taking favours from the barman who is a taciturn old bastard and you hate asking him for credit even though it is in the bar's own interest which is why you prefer tapping Pierre even if it does mean the 20 per cent extra onto the loan, but there you are, and across at the bar a few folk are waiting to be served – unsusual in itself considering the day of the week it is – which makes it difficult to signal the old cunt and when finally you do he comes over and will make it necessary to raise your voice so that every boozer in the fucking place hears you asking for tick, and for that reason alone you are somehow obliged to add to your order at the last moment, calling for three whiskies as well as the three pints of beer. Now obviously the dwarfs didnt want any fucking whisky and neither did you and there is no satisfactory explanation as to why you will have done it. But you will have done it and that is fucking that. Down on the table you thrust the drinks, right under their noses, unable to say one single word because if you do, if you so much as glance in their direction you will end up having to punch them, you will kick fuck out them, you will smash a bottle across their bastarn skulls. What you do is settle on your chair and stare at the whisky, eventually shuddering in anticipation of that horrible boke ahead, when the first drop of whisky hits at your tastebuds, all the time knowing how the dwarfs will gulp at theirs and express an honest relish of the flavour. Moments later you have invited them back to the site.

The possibility of spare tents. Who referred to that in an absent-minded manner? The very question sends you into a reverie on the nature of dualism. Meanwhile the dwarfs are trying to stop themselves bouncing up and down on their chairs. Their studied, unclamorous display of thanks cannot be described properly. Yet you will recognise its truth. The dwarfs mean no harm. There is no side to them. They make manifest their feelings in the only way they know how. You attempt to lay the blame on their shoulders but know fine well that it is you, only you, you are to blame. All else is a fraud. Every last thing is a fraud. And on you go for another few minutes inventing different ways of saying the same thing, till finally your brain develops its own release and suddenly the noises of the pub bring you back to reality: you leap up off the chair and shout it is time to be going! if you dont leave at once the tents must no longer be available! The dwarfs will look at each other behind your back, indicating the drinks on the table and whether they swallow what remains or not can never be known for you are already outside the door, gasping at the fresh air, ridding your lungs, freed from the toxins, clawing for the stillness, those quiet and distant sounds of the countryside, in solitude, the period of late dusk, its beauty.

But the door bangs open and clicks shut. The dwarfs are beside you, waiting in silence, gazing over the fields in the direction of the campsite, enjoying the scene, its tranquility. Now you will tell them the tent may be theirs for one night and one night only because as far as authority is concerned yours is less than fuck all if truth be told and you are really only doing this as a favour for some reason or another you are not quite sure except that you cannot take any chances because tenure does not exist here and the camping site proprietor is a funny kind of cunt who takes instant dislikes to people for no apparent reason. And come morning the pair of them must bolt the course at all costs. Either that or they must seek an interview with the proprietor himself because you can have nothing more to do with it. Sorry, but that is that. You carry on talking like this, any old rubbish will do, just so long as it offers the slim possibility of them deciding against the site. And without warning you march off down the lane, clattering your boots to keep from hearing their footsteps behind you. And what about their fucking goods and chattels you're thinking. Surely they've fucking brought some stuff with them! Are they just going to come straight down the lane after you without even having to stop off and collect a bundle of bags from beneath a fucking bush! What is it with these dwarfs you're thinking. What in the name of christ is it all about? The went-befores! This is what you're looking for. But there are no went-befores. Nor is it a matter of simple faith in you as the kind of total stranger who doesnt mind putting oneself about on behalf of a fellow human being. Not at all. What is it then? Fuck knows, you dont have an earthly. Maybe they are Christians you think, who can tell with dwarfs, when it comes down to it, one side or the other. And then, as though wafting on the breeze, one matter-of-fact voice is remarking to the other on some remote question such as the itness of the stars and since you will have come in at the end and not really heard the context you'll toss out some daft comment such as the funny thing about stars is you never hear anybody remarking on them in a specific sense but only as some kind of vaguely collective unity viz O look at the stars! But never O look at that particular star up there to the right hand side of the bastarn moon. And then the reply you receive: What about the Pole Star? You never heard of the Pole Star? Or the Plowe, what about the Plowe? The Plowe by christ! But you have been so tightly, so tightly, so — knotted, so tightly knotted inside that you havent a fucking clue at all about the Plowe at all until they spell it out as p-l-o-u-g-h and then you remember all about the fucking thing but in so exasperated a fashion you will demand to know why it is called the Plough and not just plain ordinary plough plural since there is a fucking cluster of the bastards — jesus christ you're shouting why do they not say there's plough instead of fucking the Plough. And before you know where you are you're off and charging home to the tent. Home to the tent. What a fraud. This tent was never home. You only labelled it home for some fanciful notion you had about watering holes and final resting places. In fact, this tent in which you are currently dwelling is situated on a camping site you have yet to admit is falling down about your ears. Aye, precisely, the camping site has been disintegrating: you were ignoring it, probably hoping the problem would go away. But the very presence of the dwarfs is enough to establish the reality. And for some reason you will now go off at a tangent, raving at the dwarfs on the subject of necessities; of the need to keep tents clean, of not smoking under canvas, of rolling up one's walls in the morning to let in the fresh air because everybody knows there's nothing worse than stuffy tents at the height of summer. Not so bad if you are on your tod as the likes of yourself but hopeless when there's more than one sharing. And what about the needs of the third party. On a camping site a great many people live and all it requires is one bad apple and the whole place takes a nosedive. Consider for example tidiness: it isnt a question of being fucking neat, it all has to do with hygiene. If you forget to clean your fucking pots and pans you wind up getting mice and rats and fuck knows what else. The same applies to the swimming pool. You go walking about all day in the middle of fields in your bare feet and then jump in for a swim and what happens? fucking obvious. And holidaymaking weans just run about here, there and everywhere, and there's no point telling the parents cause they just fucking look at you, and the same applies to chucking food away into the long grass, as if it's going to disappear. That is the kind of thing that happens. This is why you have to be tidy. The chores must be done. It is necessary. You glance at the dwarfs to see whether they are appreciating the point. They will be walking beside you – not exactly parallel because they dont like being forward, a couple of steps to the rear they will be. And they pause significantly while you unbolt the fence into the walking area. At this point you know you've been talking a load of rubbish. They will enjoy doing the chores. Chores shall be done without a grumble. It isnt that dwarfs enjoy chores. In fact they do not do chores because chores do not exist. Chores? what are they at all! They just see themselves as performing a lot of wee actions. They perform a list of wee actions they see as necessary if ever they are to become fully-fledged campers. Jesus christ. And now you glimpse your tent, away to the rear of the field, where you had figured isolation a certainty until the day the first holidaymaking family had arrived and pitched their one right fucking next to it, under the misapprehension some sort of prearranged order was in operation. Behind you the hinges of the gate creak as the dwarfs footer around, letting you know they are well up on country matters and are bolting the lock on the fucking fence. The door of the Ladies Washroom opens and out steps a mum. She will be a young mum and this is the end of her second week, she leaves on Saturday morning. She always wears a thin summer dress and goes about barelegged and has taken on a great tan while her husband has remained a peely wally white no matter how often he lies out in the sun on that inflatable rubber mattress. And even so, the most she has ever given you is a nodded good morning or good evening without once saying hello. And here she is bestowing a beaming smile on the dwarfs and all they do is grin idiotically. There's no fucking point any longer. You pause a moment in case she thinks you're following her and then wave your arm in the direction of the empty tents, before leaving the dwarfs to take their pick. And you walk by a roundabout path to your own, knowing that come a certain stage they should be unable to see you in the dark. And even if you're fucking luminous, so what? The dwarfs have arrived and the game is up. Your part is at an end. From hereon you have become redundant. You are no longer required. They see that you have no authority. They must do as they please, they can come or go and stay or leave. What they do has become their own affair. Aw jesus you think, they're off my back at last; and inside the tent you bury yourself beneath the pile of old blankets and just manage to set the alarm before falling completely asleep. It is Thursday night after all, and you've been tired out, up since half five in the morning and out working a twelve hour shift in the fields. Not even the dwarfs can keep you awake.

The next day is very strange indeed. Unfathomable matters are somehow in motion. Things are taking place sightly beyond arm's reach. It is peculiar. Out in the field you are smiling to yourself quite frequently. But it is no surprise to discover you have had a bad morning. The frenchmen are frowning; you arent picking your fair share of the crop. But there again, your back and shoulders are more knackered than usual and once you've had your dinner you'll make it all up in the afterrnoon session. Instead you find yourself lagging behind again. You were in a reverie. What the hell was it about? You cannot remember; it is all hazy, something to do with green fields and blue skies and walking down a sandy beach, arm in arm with a young woman dressed in a summer dress, a bikini on underneath. Now that you dwell on it you vaguely recollect having listened in on the conversation you both were having. What was it about? It was probably important. Up ahead the lorry has arrived and the frenchmen are carrying the crop across to it. Emil and Jaques are already there and loading up. Normally you would be there with them. You like to be first and seen to be doing the heavy work. Fuck it you're thinking you cannot be bothered, not today. Yet this is Friday. Glorious Friday. Of all the days this is the day, the one you get weighed in with the wages and see yourself fixed for another week. Even forming the words makes it seem ridiculous. Your trouble is you're a dreamer. You have been carrying on as though things are remaining the same. But even in the act of admitting this to yourself you are aware of the smile lurking about your mouth. The truth is you dont fucking care, you arent really bothering. If you were bothering why are you here when you could be home guarding your interests? The farmer would have given you the day off. You only had to ask. In fact, you preferred to come in and spend the day picking pomme de terres; you knew it would allow your brain to take off, it would allow you the opportunity of ignoring the dwarfs – an opportunity which you werent slow to accept. Ah well you're thinking, that's it all fucking finished now, and thank christ for that. Aye, precisely, that is what you are thinking at this very point. You will be doing nothing whatsoever. You will be stuck in the middle of a field doing nothing whatsoever. Meanwhile the frenchmen are nudging each other, wondering what is going on. Meanwhile the dwarfs are on the camping site wreaking their own particular form

of havoc. A bunch of holidaymaking dads is discussing the dreadful
condition of the place, the dreadful amenities on offer, the dreadful
state of the swimming pool into which their weans are plunging,
these bastarn television sets always conking out; supposedly sturdy
tents that keep collapsing on people's heads, a plague of moles and
field mice and all the litter abounding in the long grass and hedges
surrounding the campsite stores and cooking area, plus the broken
glass for weans' feet, it is a fucking disgrace, a disgrace. On and on
it goes, their list, lengthening, ever lengthening; the whole fucking
place is a shambles. And there in the background the dwarfs are
nodding deferentially, because somehow they are linking you to the
carry on and doing their best to stick up for you, they dont fucking
realize you arent the campsite fucking proprietor and it doesnt have
anything to do with you in the first place except insofar as you were
attempting to be a permanent resident, you were referring to the
dump as home, charging around with your head stuck in the grass,
lapsing into reveries connected with watering holes and final resting
places, while all about you things were disintegrating. The dwarfs
were only a reply. And yet, you will say, if they hadnt arrived it
wouldnt be happening. They are to blame. While you were at work
they've been charging around the site sowing seeds of discontent
among the holidaymakers. Not by intention – granted, there is no
malice, okay, you can accept that but still and all, still and all: they
have come and they have taken over. They did not know what they
were doing. They probably thought they were just being polite when
chatting to the holidaymaking dads about the semi-detached villa on
the outskirts of Burnley. They couldnt comprehend that amicable
forms of neighbourly chit chat might lead to the comparison of
mental notes concerning the so-called campsite and its so-called
amenities which are rubbish when you consider what is being
offered across on the west coast at little or no difference in cost.

   And now you know why you have not been working properly this
morning. Even your reveries were fraudulent. That other thing was
there, it was lurking in at the root, way to the rear of your brain,
at so deeply set back a place that your fucking subconscious wasnt
even aware of it. This is why you lagged behind the frenchmen, the

farmer frowning at you, wondering if you really are up to it after all. No, you didnt enjoy this morning. Normally a Friday is good but today has been terrible and you are suffering, you are, no point denying it. And now a deputation is being formed by the holiday-making mums and dads to march right in and confront the camping site proprietor first thing tomorrow morning. And this camping site proprietor … Camping site proprietor! what a joke. Because he owns a camping site they call him that. He knows next to nothing about camping sites. The whole kit and caboodle would have collapsed weeks ago if you hadnt been dropping hints via the wee woman from the village about all the day-to-day work and upkeep required. Between the two of you you kept the place going. Now she's fucked off and left you to it. But what more could be done, you're saying, what more could be done!

Then collecting your wages later, you were aware of a peculiar diffidence on the part of the farmer when he passed you the envelope. How come he never looked you in the eye? And the frenchmen hanging back, waiting for you to leave before collecting theirs, as though they dont want to be tainted by the bad luck surrounding you. But it isnt bad luck. That is what you want to say, it's only circumstances. Things get out of control. That is what happens in life. No big deal. Only you feel like a beer now, instead of going home first to have a wash and change the clothes. The outside tap round the side of the barn, fuck it, give the head and shoulders a splash, then straight to the pub man that is where you'll be heading. You need a drink, and the way you've been suffering you're entitled to one. The fucking dwarfs! You smile to yourself, because it is amazing how they can come and just take over. Funny. There you are in foreign climes, the only guy in the entire vicinity, you are the only one, you. Then you arent. Just when you think you have everything fixed, just when you do, when you do have everything fixed – almost everything, bang, finished, all gone, all of it, fucking everything.

You have been walking, walking a while, walking a long while, walked way beyond the village pub, way way beyond. A car has whizzed by and as its sound decreased you became aware of it and thus of yourself there walking, just walking. Now here you are.

What will you do? return to the pub or continue walking; in forty five more minutes you could be in town – less should a bus appear. On this part of the island buses are infrequent but they do appear now and again. Or you could thumb a lift, or just enjoy the walk for the rest of the road. It is a nice day, and a nice day for walking, the kind of day you enjoy so much, working in the fields and returning home to the site, cooking a few spuds, lazily, not bothering much about anything; the cries of the weans from the swimming pool and play area, the holidaymaking parents sitting outside their tents relaxing after the evening repast, music quietly in the background, Friday night. And you will return to the pub. You still have to weigh in Pierre with the couple of quid you borrowed earlier in the week. And anyway, you arent dressed for the town, still in the working togs. Different if you had gone home first and had a decent wash and shave and so on but you didnt do that. In fact, this entire carry on about going into town, will you or wont you, it is more than familiar it is mauvaise foi fucking bad faith shite, that is what it is. You always mean to go into town, you never fucking get there. No wonder the irritated sigh.

You have to pause, keeping in to the side of the road as a pair of cyclists pass, and you almost fall into the ditch to avoid the bastards because they dont even bother it is you, you have to do it, otherwise you would have got fucking knocked down. You stay on the grass by the side of the ditch, enjoying the seat, take out the tobacco, roll a smoke. It is true that you've been meaning to go into town on a more regular basis. Just the time it takes getting back from work to the campsite, washing and cooking and all the rest of it, getting yourself ready, dressed and stuff, then hoofing it down the lane to the junction in the offchance a bus happens along – usually you've just missed one and cross the road to the pub to pass the time then before you know where you are, who cares about buses. In future you'll make more of an effort, definitely. Local bars are all very well. A change is as good as a rest. Seeing the same old faces all the time. Especially that cunt of a barman who seems in the wrong job altogether. What is it with him at all the way he serves people? If he doesnt like dishing out booze to folk he shouldnt work in a fucking pub. That superior smile on his coupon. How come they always have them? barmen, superior smiles. No wonder you always

jesus christ the two quid! you owe him two quid! You forgot about that, the two quid you owe him. But it wasnt him it was the brewery, he was just the fucking link; he gave you the money out the till but it was the brewery's money. So you have to return him the dough. If you go to the local pub the first two quid is his. Fucking dwarfs of course they'll be there as well, they'll be in the bar waiting. They've probably been out looking for you, because they are loyal and thoughtful to others – and they want to advise you of the camp-site shenanigans, the irate dads' deputation for tomorrow morning, their petitions and so on. It isnt a question of them not wanting you to think they're working behind your back because that never occurs to them because they arent, they are entirely above board. They only want to fill you in on the details. Amazing they'll say, these poor holidaymakers, we never knew it was that bad but from what they are telling us it is really dreadful, and Tommy Jackson – he's from Burnley, a nice fellow, lovely wife he's got and a couple of smashing weans; we've taught them to swim already, and go a bike – Tommy has been telling us about the amenities, really fucking dreadful so they are, did you know?

Did you know! What a joke, did you know. No you say, you didnt. And they look at each other as though joined at the nose. They are standing by where you now are sitting. They have full pints of beer in their hands. A couple of the holidaymaking dads guessed they were skint and offered them a couple of quid till they landed their first job. They didnt ask, they were offered. And one of the holidaymaking mums has been feeding them all day. After the chores they were getting through she thought they deserved it. All day they've been at it, on behalf of one and all, going hammer and tongs, you should have seen them, cleaning up the entire place, charging about here, there and everywhere, mending fuses, laying concrete, fixing televisions, trawling the swimming pool for slugs and dead insects, drowned rodents and accident-prone fucking moles. They even fixed an appointment with the camping site proprietor for tomorrow morning's deputation. Aye, they just marched up to the front door of the house, and chapped it, and the cunt answered, he answered. According to rumour he's going to offer them the job of running the campsite shop if the wee woman from the village never returns. Oh but no no they say, they can never do that, they would far rather the wee woman did return and they're going to charge down the village first thing Monday morning and drag her back if need be, all for the good of everybody. They reckon she'll listen to reason. She will, she'll invite them in for their fucking breakfast. It really is funny the way it works. At the same time you have to admire them. Do they have something special about them? Surely they must! What is it they've got? Because they've definitely got something. There's Pierre too, taciturn loanshark bastard, telling a couple of frenchmen to squeeze up so the dwarfs can sit down at the domino table. Did you hear right! Sit down at the domino table! Aye, fucking Pierre. The dwarfs are trying not to appear too keen in case you're offended, maybe you were expecting the invitation and here it is gone to them. Is that fair? Then somebody asks if they want to sit in for a hand and of course they do because back where they come from they played the game on a regular basis, so thanks very much and they will, if nobody's got any objections? And who would have, except you, except you cant think of any, except just life, life itself.

You have to hand it to the wee bastards. You can only smile, shaking your head in wonder. In fact you would probably quite like them if you werent so fucking . . . so fucking . . . so fucking what? You are frowning now: stop frowning. There they are right beside you, taking the spectators' part in the game as energetically as any of the frenchmen, grinning and yapping away, gesticulating to their hearts' content, and smiling at you because you smiled at them. You did. But they wont suspect your smiling really is to them, they probably think you're just glad to be alive. Two of the holidaymaking dads have entered the bar — Desmond and Fred — and are trying to attract the dwarfs' attention. They are supposed to be meeting them for a pint but now when they spot the pair surrounded by locals they become sheepish and dont want to be pushy although at the same time they are secretly proud to know them — personal acquaintance with the locals usually produces that effect. In a couple of minutes one of the dads will arrive with two pints of beautiful Guinness. He has bought them for the dwarfs. He walks with determined nonchalance, sets the pints on the ledge beneath the custom-built domino table. For the sake of politeness he pauses to study the game. Nobody notices. After a decent interval a dwarf glances upwards and says, Ta Desmond, then returns his attention to the dominoes. But then he glances back: O by the way, how's the wee boy? is his knee any better? The wee boy cut his knee earlier on apparently; he fell in the long grass round the back of his tent, landed on a shard of glass apparently, or a fucking nail, a rusty one. Aw he's fine now, says the holidaymaker, last I saw he was plunging into the swimming pool. O and by the way, thanks for cleaning it out. No danger pal, says the dwarf. The holidaymaker returns to his mate at the bar who is doing his best to attract the dwarfs' attention. He manages it, and gives them a wave and a cheery smile. What a con! You cannot believe guys fall for this sort of shite but holidaymakers do. You're wanting to yell across to them, It is shite, dont fall for it! But for one reason or another you dont bother. You dont have the fucking energy. But aside from that, aside from that you feel more like laughing, at the sheer effrontery because really, it isnt funny, not remotely. You clear your throat, move your shoulders, sip at your own beer, calming yourself, at least trying to – it would be pointless doing anything daft. Aye, suddenly you find yourself capable of that. It's because the place is so crowded. There arent enough seats to go round. Friday night of course, the start of the weekend, the place hoaching with holiday-makers, from all over. Many have only just stepped off the boat, their own boat. You spot them immediately because of how they look. The ordinary holidaymakers are fine, it's just these weekend boat sailors you're opposed to. You couldnt mistake the loud-mouthed bastards the way they stand there gabbing, letting everybody know who they are. They think they own the fucking place. Another reason for making more of an effort to get into town in future, especially Friday nights, far better than the village local. You have turned to the dwarfs and begun telling them about this. They nod. They are not a hundred percent interested, hardly at all in fact; their real interest is the domino game. You pause while talking to them and they dont

even notice. You smile ruefully. Emil smiles back at you. He is one of
the players and thinks your smile is linked to the bad domino he has
just played. His smile is also rueful; he shakes his head and mutters
something in french, about to lose the game.

When it ends you go for another pint and ask for a whisky as
well; as an afterthought you buy whiskies for the dwarfs, because
they already have their fresh pints lying. The old barman looks at you.
There is something about the look, a puzzled quality, and not just
the additional whiskies. For a moment you think you've misjudged
the man; maybe he just has that kind of face, he isnt really a taciturn
old bastard. How would you like to be cooped up all day yourself,
having to serve these fucking boat sailors with drink! No joke. When
the barman returns with your change you smile but he ignores you,
old cunt that he is, so that's him won again. From now on you are
definitely going to town, starting from tomorrow; as soon as you
finish work you're going straight home for a wash and a shave and
a complete change of clothes. No question. There can be no excuse
either because Saturdays you only work the eight hour shift. You lift
your tray of drinks and catch sight of the old barman, he's staring
into space while pouring a pint for a holidaymaker. Even that staring
he does, it's in the direction opposite the guy. He wont even look
at him. That is out of order. Even if the job is bad as that why take it
out on the customer? Far better to resign, just fucking leave. One of
these days a disgruntled party's going to stick one on the old cunt's
chin and it might well be you, that's what you're thinking, and the
thought has you smiling then laughing, okay quietly, but you have to
clear your throat to stop it. The dwarfs look at you, politely. Aye, you
say, and begin telling them about a funny thing that happened while
you were out in the field the other day. They are interested to hear.
But a lot of funny things do happen. All in all there are a lot worse
jobs than the old pomme de terres, and you tell the dwarfs that, the
fresh air and so on, there's a lot to be said for it. Even if jobs were
plentiful, you reckon you would still be out there picking spuds. Of
course there isnt much choice nowadays. Not now there isnt. The
dwarfs nod. You're glad they appreciate the point because a few folk
land in this place expecting the farmers to be queuing up to offer

them work. The same applies to roofs over the head. A great many cunts land here thinking it's all straightforward and it isnt, nowhere near. Okay it used to be but not nowadays. If you dont get things fixed early you're bang in trouble. It's knowing the ins and outs. If you do that then okay, you have to consider the eventualities, sort out what is possible from what is not possible. It's always surprising the number of folk who cant do that. Take yourself for instance, when you first landed on these shores you had your eyes open, none of that romantic shite about tropical paradises, you knew you had to graft; it was all down to you. The one thing you've learned in this life: if you want to do something then do it yourself because no cunt's going to do it for you. What are you kidding! That's a fucking beauty! You could laugh aloud at that. But you dont. What you do is raise your glass and sip slowly, gazing at the dwarfs over the rim. And they are gazing back at you. They have been listening. They are next in line for the domino game and are wanting to return their attention to there but are unsure whether they should or not. And they make their decision; they continue gazing at you. They expect something. You are to speak. What are you to say? They are waiting. What is it you …

O jesus.

It will be a beautiful summer's evening. One of those where you get that amazing expanse of sky and then when it darkens a shade you see the stars, an infinity of them. It always looks special when you're on an island and standing looking from the middle of a field; the sky, it's like a blanket or something, with thousands and millions of shining stars and each moment you witness the thing another one explodes into life. It is amazing. Yet so many people dont even bother looking at the stars. They come to a place like this and go walking about with their head stuck in the grass. The dwarfs arent like that. This much you can say. They genuinely appreciate the value of things, same as yourself. If you have any criticisms to make it concerns their naivety. Not in the ordinary sense, they certainly arent naive – otherwise they wouldnt be here and making a go of things as well as they are – no, it has more to do with faith or something. The way they look upon you for instance; you can understand why they regard you so highly but you'd advise against this in future.

Christ, you have to stop talking. You shake your head. There's a lump in your throat. You stare at your whisky, not wanting to be seen, not at this moment.

The dwarfs have coughed, delicately, shifting on their chairs so they cannot see you without turning their heads. They are good guys. They are thoughtful and they are fucking loyal. People from your place are like that. You dont care what anybody says. That is the fucking god's truth. Yet it is funny how it happens, and you smile when you offer them your job. You are not a hundred percent certain the farmer'll take them on because there is only one of you and two of them. But you reckon they should give it a try. They could do worse. And once the farmer sees how well they get on with the frenchmen – because they do get on with the frenchmen, much better than you. The same goes for the holidaymakers. There are other problems – well, not really problems, more to do with irksome chores. Then you have the deputation re bad amenities and fraudulent advertising in holiday brochures. The most important thing to remember is the campsite proprietor himself. He is the fucking danger, the unstable factor. Whatever you do you must never put the jitters into him. He is so fucking incompetent, and so very aware of being incompetent, that he will run a mile the first chance he gets. You have to kid him on. You have to drag him along by the nose, just tug, gently. Or else he'll run for cover. He'll close down the site and head for the mainland. You've seen cunts like him before and so have the dwarfs. There is no real need to tell them, you just thought to mention it.

O, and the holidaymakers, there is quite a bit to be said about them and you start in on that for a time, until you notice the dwarfs have turned their heads from you; the domino game is finishing and they are on the alert. The excitement mounts and people are pressing in. How noisy it all is. Too fucking noisy. Friday night of course, that is what you're thinking, these boat sailor bastards and their constant yap yap yapping. They seem to have bribed the old barman to turn the volume up on the jukebox. A couple of the females are dancing a bit while the males sip at their half pint shandies.

It wont be long till you apply the method. This is it: a dwarf will rise to his feet to go to the bar for a round of drinks and while manoeuvering his way through the boat sailors will accidentally rub against a dancing female, and one of the males will pass a comment. One thing leads to another. The upshot is that you, being the tallest member of the present company, will challenge the tallest boat sailor to go to the boxing games. At this a great tumult shall occasion. People are on all sides of you, many of whom you recognise. They are trying to paw at you, excited by the drama ahead. You hear them discuss this, that and the next thing with some of the female boat sailors, trying to play matters down. But the males arent allowing it. They want to prove themselves, not just with the females but with the locals. This is it about these fucking boat sailors, they act as if they own the place when in reality they are most insecure and hate it when they enter village bars like this one, and receive cheek from sarcastic barmen while at the same time the females are getting ogled by the regulars – not just frenchmen. You can hear the holidaymakers attempting to pacify the combatants, to no avail, and then a shrill though distinct voice, vaguely familiar, rises above the herd, advocating a more sporting contest. Boxing is all very well but might be a trifle one-sided! What about something less violent? maybe a swim or some fucking thing. Great you shout and make a lunge at the tallest boat sailor: Me and you outside in the fucking Ocean ya bastard! And this does the trick. The silence lasts several moments before the tumult continues – it appears to be a kind of vote. It is a vote. A loud cheer goes up when a voice calls: Carried! And then by your side you feel hands tapping your shoulder in a furtive way; it's the dwarfs, attempting to dissuade you! Is this a contradiction? maybe a paradox, you arent sure, there isnt time, you only can look at them. No! they cry, you shouldnt be swimming on a night like this, not with all that beer and whisky slopping around in your belly. Out my road, you shout, out my road. A couple of holidaymakers are there as well, including the young mother in her summer dress, her slim shoulders and soft rounded breasts, looking so worried, so worried, really, her hand to the side of her mouth and clutching her wee white hankie: will you return from the deep!

Who gives a fuck, that's what you're thinking, except why be huffy why be huffy, if she's there she's there. Jesus christ! But too late, too fucking late you're shouting too fucking late. You're just wanting out there; nothing else matters; nothing. Where's that fucking boat sailor who insulted your wee pal the dwarf? that's what you're wanting to know. He's waiting outside with his cronies. Aye and you might have guessed, the cunt's got a pair of swimming trunks, bona fide ones out a sports shop. Ah well. And there's the frenchmen laying bets – fucking Pierre, he's making a book on survival – and glancing with interest as you go scurrying by, trying to keep up with the long striding onlookers. That giant boat sailor bastard's already out there with a couple of his shipmates: Ahoy ya cunt. One of them's testing the temperature of the Ocean and he's saying: Not as cold as when you swam the fucking channel Bertie! Aw good, says the boat sailor, glad to hear it. You're straightening your shoulders and marching past him, way beyond, way way beyond, the Ocean lapping at your ankles. You pause to kick off your working boots. You can hear indistinct voices from the shore. Is it cheers you wonder? Who cares you say, and when the water rises up and beyond your knees you plunge in and begin a hectic breaststroke in a direction sou' sou'-westerly.

Manufactured in Paris

Whole days you spend walking about the dump looking for one and all you get's sore feet. I'm fucking sick of it. Sweaty bastarn feet. I went about without socks for a spell and the sweat was worse, streams in my shoes. Shoes! no point calling them shoes. Seen better efforts on a – christ knows what. Cant make you a pair of shoes these days. More comfort walking about in a pair of mailbags. A while ago I was passing a piece of waste ground where a few guys were kicking a ball about. On I went. We got a game going. Not a bad game. I kicked the stuffing out my shoes but. The seams split. Everybastarnthing split. Cutting back down the road with the soles flapping and that. And I had no spare pairs either by christ nothing, nothing at all. Then I found a pair of boots next to a pillarbox. This pair of boots had been Manufactured in Paris. Paris by christ. They lasted me for months too. Felt like they were mine from the start. I had been trying to pawn a suit that day. No cunt would take it. We dont take clothes these days is what they all said. Tramped all over the dump. Nothing. Not a bad suit as well. This is a funny thing about London. Glasgow – Glasgow is getting as bad right enough. They still take clothes but the price they give you's pathetic. I once spent forty-eight quid on a suit and when I took it along they offered me three for it. Three quid. Less than four months old by christ. A fine suit too. 14 ounce cloth and cut to my own specifications. The trimmings. That suit had the lot. I always liked suits. Used to spend a fortune on the bastards. Foolish. I gave it all up. It was a heatwave then as well right enough but an honest decision nevertheless.

The Place!

Deep water. I want to float through breakers and over breastrok-ing across uplifted by them. This is what I need. And upon the deep open sea. Freshwater wont do. Where are the breakers in fresh-water. None. You dont fucking get them. I want to be by a sheer rockface. The steep descent to reach the sea where at hightide the caves are inaccessible by foot alone. I have to startle birds in their nests from within the caves. At hightide the rockplunge into the deep. That is what I want. That. I can swim fine and I can swim fine at my own pace and I have no illusions about my prowess. I'm not getting fucked about any longer.

There is a place I know on the coast. I cant go there. It is not in reach. The remains of a Druid cemetry close by, accounts for a few tourists. The tourists never visit the Place. Maybe they do. But it isnt a real reason for not going. There are real reasons, real reasons. My christ what a find this place was. I climbed down a dangerous part of the rockface. Right down and disregarding mostly all I know of climbing down the dangerous parts. Only perhaps 25 feet. The tide was in. I wanted to fall in. I wanted to dive in. I did not know if it was safe to dive in. If there were rocks jutting beneath the surface. So I did not want to dive in. I wanted to fall in and find out whether it was safe for diving. But if I fell onto submerged rocks I might have been killed so I did not want to fall in at all for fuck sake which is why I clung at shallow clumps of weedgrass, loose slate; and it was holding fast, supporting me, the weight. I kept getting glimpses of the caves. Impossible to reach at hightide except by swimming. When I got down to where I could only go I saw the rocks in the depth and had to get away at that moment seeing the rocks there I had to get away at once and each grain of matter was now loosening on my touch my toes cramped and I had to cling on this loose stuff applying no none absolutely no pressure at all but just balancing there with the toes cramped in this slight crevice.

A Nightboilerman's notes

The bunker faces outwards, away to the far corner of the ground surface area. When it requires replenishing (twice nightly) I push the bogey out into the corridor and through the rearmost swing doors, down the steep incline onto the pathway by the canal, along to where the coalmountains pile some thirty yards from the embankment. It is good to walk here, the buckled rattle of the bogey wheels only emphasizing the absence of noise. The Nightoutsideman has charge of this area. I used to envy him. His job has seemed always so straightforward in comparison to this one of mine. He sits on his chair to the side of his hut door, gazing to the sky or to the canal. I walk past him but he does not look across, not until he hears that first strike of my shovel into the coal, when he turns and waves.

It takes 4 bogey loads to replenish the bunker. I could manage it with 3 but the incline up into the factory is too steep to push the bogey comfortably if fully laden. And there is no need to rush. This part of the shift I like. Once the 4th load is in the bogey I leave it standing and go over to have a smoke with the Nightoutsideman. We exchange nods. I lean my back against the wall on the other side of the hut door from him; sometimes I lower myself down to sit on my heels. Due to the configuration of warehouse and factory buildings there is never any wind here (a very very slight breeze, but only occasionally) and the canal is still, its water black and sudsy, the grey foam spreading out from its banks.

He will have been waiting for me to arrive before making his next cigarette. He used to make one for me but I prefer my own. I strike the match; while I am exhaling on the first draw I flick the match out onto the canal, watching for its smoke but there never is any; if there is I havent been able to see it. He raises his eyebrows, a brief smile. He smiles a lot, speaks very rarely; he just likes to sit there watching the things happen. Most of the buildings are unoccupied during the night and their differing shapes and shadows, the shades of black and grey, red-tinged. Now and then he will gesture at the sky, at the bend in the canal, sideways at one of the buildings, to the one where jets of steam issue suddenly from escape pipes, and to high up in the same building, the large windows where headlike shapes appear frequently. I never quite grasp what he is on about, the meaning of the gesture, but it probably has to do with plain truths, and I nod in reply, as though acknowledging a contrast. Then when I finish the smoke I flick the dowp out onto the canal, listening for the plop that never comes (which never could come, not in any canal). I wait on a few moments, before going to get the bogey. I like this last push up the incline, that rutted point near the top where the wheels seem to be jamming and the bogey halts and

I cannot hold it any longer! All my strength has gone! The load is going to roll back down and crash into the canal!

then I grin, breathe deeply and shove, continuing on upwards and through the rubber swing doors into the corridor, still grinning.

I have charge of the boilers. Their bodies are situated in the basement and their mouths range the ground surface area, sealed off by solid square hatches with set-in rings. The floor is made of specially-treated cast-iron plating so that although it is still very hot it is never too hot such that it is impossible for a human being to walk upon when wearing special boots (metal studded and perhaps the uppers are of a special substance?).

When I arrive with the 4th load of coal I wheel the bogey past the bunker and go straight across to begin the stoking. I have a crowbar to wedge inside the rings to wedge up the hatches which will settle at an angle of 100°. With the hatch raised the heat and light from the

boiler is very tremendous and I have to avert my face while stoking.
Asbestos gloves are there to be used if so required but experienced
workers manage without them, taking care not to touch the circular
metal sections of the shovel. It is habit now and I cannot recall the
last time my hands burnt. There is an interesting phenomenon that
a child might like to see: this is the coaldust dropping from my shovel
during the stoking procedure; it ignites simultaneously to touching the ground surface area so that countless tiny fires are always
blazing, and it looks startling (diamonds that sparkle).

Then I have finished and kick down the hatch, and that thud of
impact separating the loud roaring of the open boiler from the dull
roaring of the closed boiler that I can never quite anticipate. And
I move onto the next. Finally, when I have fed them all, I wheel off the
bogey to its position by the bunker then return with the wirebrush
to sweep clean the ground surface. Coalbits will be lying smoulder-
ing or burning nearby the hatches; I sweep them straight across this
floor and into the water trench next to the basement entrance.
Towards the end of the shift I rake out the trench and use the
gathered embers and dross on the last stoke. Whenever I forget to
do this the trench is full of dross when I arrive next evening. The
Dayboilerman is responsible. He is known for his moods. This is his
way of reminding me not to do it again.

From a distance the entrance to the basement resembles another
boilermouth but it is set away to the side of the ground surface
area and its hatch is permanently raised. There is an internal ladder
reaching down from the mouth, the top ends welded onto the
inside panel of the hatch. I enjoy descending. I grip either side
with both hands, sometimes scurrying down to break the existing
speed record! Other times I go very very slowly, stepping carefully,
deliberately, as though engaged upon ultra-serious business concerning submarines and missiles. I can be standing watching myself
from way over beyond the bunker, seeing my head sink from view,
vanishing, wondering if it cracked against the edge of the metal
plated floor but no; always I just avoid that by the briefest margin

possible, gglullp, gone. Then I poke out my head again. Or maybe remain exactly there, beneath the surface, counting 25 and only then shall I reappear, and back down immediately.

Nowadays I appreciate no task more than those that have me down in the basement. It did use to have its frightening aspects but my imagination was to blame. The black holes is the best example. I would step past them and pretend they were not there; or if they were, that I was not particularly bothered by them. This was daft and I knew it was daft but I was working out a method of conquering myself, and came to realize that. In those days I was having to force myself to enter the basement. I discussed the matter inwardly; these black holes, they are ordinary black holes, ordinary in the sense that they are man-made, they only exist because of the way the walls have been designed. They also exist as they do, these black holes, because of the effect the lighting system produces on the boiler-bodies: permanent shadows. These permanent shadows amount to a creation.

The basement is a sealed unit, built to accomodate the boilers; the one entrance/exit is by way of the welded ladder. Firstly the boilers were sited then they built the basement, and the rest of the building. It took me a while to understand that fully. And when I had I think I was either beyond my fear or well on the road to this. It was pretty bad at the time. I had to force myself to sit beside them, the holes, facing away from them, not to see them, not without turning my head. I would sit like that for ages thinking of horrible things but not being aware of this until later, sometimes much later, when walking home in the morning. There was an occasion the Dayboilerman found me in that seated position. The sound of his studded boots on the steps of the ladder had reached me but could scarcely correspond to anything I knew so that I wasnt really aware of it beyond my thoughts. Then he was there and his eyes staring as though seeing a ghost for the first time, about to collapse with a heart attack. Yet he had been looking for me. I failed to clock out at the gate and the Yard-Timekeeper asked that he might check for me, if I was anywhere (if I was anywhere; I was anywhere). So he was looking for me and when he found me reacted as though I was the last thing he expected to find sitting there. He told people I looked like a zombie. A zombie! But eventually this made me realize about the Dayboilerman that he had never managed to conquer himself. He had been nervous, very nervous indeed. What would he find! He had been scared. The controls for the basement lighting are on the wall behind the welded ladder that they may be reached before reaching the bottom but this lighting is supposed to be kept on permanently. I think the reason for this has to do with the idea of one man being down and then another man coming down without realizing that the first is there, so returning back up onto ground floor level while switching off the lighting controls, leaving the first man in blackness. That would be a horrible thing for someone new in the job. But I admit here and now that I do play around with these controls, sometimes leaving the lighting in off-mode during the periods I'm away from the basement. I think about how it all 'looks' down there, different things. Also that incredible sensation to come, when switching the lighting back on again. I go stepping off the ladder with my back to the inner wall, facing away from the shaft of light above, right out into the blackness, stepping into there. Occasionally I shall walk 3 or 4 (at the most 5) paces until that feeling of narrowness has me stock-still and trying to reflect on a variety of matters, maybe wondering how it would be having to work in such conditions forever (a miner whose lamp keeps going out?). And I continue standing there, thinking different things, then slowly but surely I notice I am moving back the way, sensing the approach of that strange feeling of being buried in cotton wool and I am turning to reach for the controls calmly, not panicking at all, only to get my bearings from the shaft of light through the entrance hatchway. And I do reach them, and the lighting is immediate throughout the basement, the noise of everything now audible apparently for the first time, that deep deep humming, humming (light gives sound).

The boilerbodies dominate the basement. I can stand watching them. They are so large. They appear so to me. The rigidity of their shadows, falling or setting upon each other. It seems as though your eyes are blurring. Between the boilerbodies a complex of narrow passageways lies. These are wide enough for a man to pass along carrying a crate of cinders, a rake and shovel. I used to think a bogey might be adapted to fit the passageways but this is not at all necessary. This idea may only have occurred to me because of move-able objects, thinking it would be good to have one, a thing to move in the midst of the fixation, the fixed eternal. In the basement there are 4 implements; the 2 crates, the rake, the shovel. Also there are 2 boilersuits that must be kept in the basement, 1 for myself and 1 for the Dayboilerman. If we require to wear boilersuits on the ground surface or outside areas then we must supply our own. I also have a towel which I keep here below. Although the atmosphere is not stifling it is akin to tropical. I think of equatorial forests full of peculiar plants and plantlife; gigantic flowers with brightly coloured buds the size of oranges hanging down the middle; scaly immoveable creatures, and that constant dripping, almost a sluicing sound. Yet there is no dripping in the basement. I have never found any. There is water in the trenches of course which surround the bottom of the boilerbodies. There are no drip-trails into them. Cinders and dross fall through escape channels into the trenches and I rake these out into the larger of the 2 crates and carry this to the foot of the welded ladder, dumping them into the smaller crate which is designed to be push-lifted up through the hatch. I perform this function towards the end of the shift, in preparation for the final stoke. This smaller crate fits snugly up through the hatch and cannot lurch sideways. I lift the crate to waist-height then continue the operation by pushing it upwards, using the welded ladder for leverage. The larger crate never leaves the basement. I enjoy carrying it between the boilerbodies. I take different routes and go quickly or slowly, sometimes very very slowly, studying my boots as they land at that point on the passageway nearest the trench. Even though I work naked I continue to wear the boots. I tried these actions barefoot but the edges of the trenches get quite slippy while I'm raking out the cinders; staying on my feet becomes hazardous, and it is not easy to walk – also a daft thing, I was being continually tempted into the water, just to dip my feet, I wanted to dip them, so very tempting, but if I had succumbed to that I would maybe have gone in for a swim! the heels touching the surface of the water, entering, submerging, creeping beyond my ankles, and the angled slope of the trenches, encountering this, and the sliding downwards, these channels beneath the bottom of each boilerbody.

The trenches narrow somewhere on that downward slope such that cinders become stuck, and stuck fast; there seem a great many crannies. I know most of these through my use of the rake on the daily basis. This part of the job is good, the raking noise and my own silence, that clung of the rakehead below the surface of the water on the sides of the trench, the scraping sound of its teeth in the crannies. I could have expected both that and the sense of touch to grate on me but they dont, perhaps because they come from outside of me altogether. I work silently, and in silence. The idea of the work noise is not easy, how it would appear to some-one (not the Dayboilerman) poking his head down through the hatch, from where I could never be seen because of the shapes and shadows, seeing how all the objects and everything are so stationary, just taking it for granted for a spell, that lack of movement, suggest-ing peace, while not being conscious of any other thing, not until that moment he has become aware of an unexpected sound or noise, but rhythmic; after a moment the onlooker would react by snorting, perhaps giving himself a telling-off for being so daft, and then he would climb back up and out as quickly as he could go, even knocking his shin on the sharp edges of the metal plates, in desperation yet maintaining the pretence that he is not at all bothered by it, any of it.

But nobody from outside ever comes down into the basement. Firstly the ground surface area needs to be crossed and it cannot be crossed without special footwear. If anybody wishes to attract my attention they either shout or batter the floor with a crowbar. It happens only rarely and I seldom respond since it is only to advise me that the pressure isnt being maintained. This I discover myself because of the safety precautions. I might be wrong not to respond. I sometimes wonder whether to ask the Dayboilerman what he does, but I dont think he does anything. His perception of the job will differ radically from mine. It cannot be avoided, constant days and constant nights, we each have our own distractions. Yes, I can still be distracted. This is essential to the work. But I cannot be distracted against my wishes. If I think of things they must be things I wish to think of.

I used to make myself sit by the black hole farthest from the entrance; it lies on the same side but to reach it I must walk to the wall opposite the welded ladder then follow the passageway there, right around and into the deepest corner. I brought the boilersuit to sit on and the towel to cover my shoulders while leaning back to the wall, then I lit the cigarette. Smoking is frowned upon down here but I've always done it; I really enjoy it, finishing a particular part of the work and sitting down calmly, not methodically, and lighting one. Sometimes when I sit down I leave the cigarettes and matches beside me for a while before smoking; other times I'm smoking even before sitting down. One thing I did in the early days, I pushed the matches and the cigarettes inside the black hole. I sat there for a long period afterwards, till finally I knelt and withdrew them without looking in, just using my hand to feel around.

There is nothing extraordinary about these black holes, they are cavities and short tunnels. I found them of interest because they had never been seen into since the factory's original construction. I still find the idea quite interesting. When I first found them I thought they were just inshots, little gaps, and I sat by them not bothering. Then one night after sitting a while I suddenly was kneeling down and peering in and I couldnt see anything, nothing at all. I struck a match and the light scarcely penetrated. It was strange, I had to push in my hand, and discovered the wall and the tunnel veering off, it veered off at a tangent. I could have brought in a torch or candle and a mirror maybe, but I never did. If I remember correctly I was wanting to check the dimensions of the wall in relation to the cavity and tunnel. I knew it had to be a kind of double wall, probably a triple one, as part of the safety precautions. I went round by the canal pathway to look at the outside of the building but that told me nothing. On this particular side of the factory the pathway only goes along a few yards before narrowing and tapering out altogether, with the wall going straight down into the water.

There were quite a lot of things about it that bothered me at the time but nowadays it all seems hazy. But I think the main factor must connect to the idea of isolation, maybe bringing on a form of deprivation. It wasnt good when I had to sit by the black holes at first; some of my imaginings were horrible. I just had to stick it out and conquer myself. I had to succeed and I did succeed. It taught me a lot about myself and has given me confidence. Sometimes I feel a bit smug, as if I've reached a higher level than the others in the factory; but I dont speak to many of them, I just get on and do the job, enjoying its various aspects.

The City Slicker and The Barmaid

I came to someplace a few miles south of the Welsh border and with luck managed to rent a tent on a farm. Not a real campsite. I was the one mug living in the place and could only stay on condition I completed certain set tasks such as pointing barn walls and driving tractors full of rubbish. Whenever the farmer was away on business I had to guide his ramshackle lorry into the village.

I also received cash for these tasks.

The tent was pitched in a grassy bit of ground next to a cobbled courtyard covered in country manure shite, hay and mud. Dirty mud as opposed to healthy stuff. The grass was long in the surrounding field. In the barn nearest the tent big rats jumped about getting fat on the hay and feed stored there. I discovered paw marks on the grease in my frying pan. This proves the rats found a way into the tent though the farmer refused to believe me. He thought I was a moaner. During the night I liked to sit at the top end of the mattress with a bottle in my hand waiting for a wee animal to creep in. Then the hedge surrounding the field was full of beetles and all manner of flying insects. When I lit my candle they broke in through rips in the canvas, perched from the roof till I fell asleep then came zooming down on me, eating my blood and knocking their knees in my hair. I was always wakening in the middle of the night scratching and clawing at my skalp and eyebrows; also the lobes of my ears, how come the lobes of my ears?

The actual farm animals themselves did not worry me. Although after sundown a pack of cows used to try and sniff me on my way home from the village pub. There were all these lanes to walk down and usually I took a shortcut through a couple of fields. These cows came wastling along at my back without a sound bar the shshsh of their smelly tails. I walked slowly, kidding on it was okay, but it wasnt and I felt like dashing headlong to the tent, but then these guyropes and metal spike things I kept tripping over and twice I fell right on top of the tent. Plus too my boots, all spattered and saturated with dew and whatever else, what a mess. I took them off at the entrance, seated on the so-called groundsheet with the doorflap open. And all the insects flew in from the hedges. The floor inside the tent was always covered in clumps of grass, dung too at times, the colour of baked seaweed. Earwigs crawled the walls searching for ears to crawl in, then the ants, ants were everywhere. I closed my eyes at night thinking "spiders, thank christ for spiders".

No sleeping bag. Terrible itchy exarmy blankets to go with the mattress, hired from the farmer's wife and deducted from my wage at source. Of course my feet stuck out at the bottom and I can never sleep wearing socks, even if I had any.

The farmhands were continually cracking jokes in Oi Bee accents at my expense. I would laugh, or stare. Other times I replied in aggressive accents of my own which got me nowhere since they pretended not to understand what I was saying. Because I drove the lorry I was accorded a certain respect. In the local den of a pub I was known as Jock the Driver. The previous driver was an Irishman who worked seven years on this farm till one Saturday night he went out for a pish round the back of the bar. It was the last they ever saw of him. A man to admire.

The guys working beside me were yesmen to the core. Carried tales about each other to the farmer and even to me if the farmer was off on business. They spent entire days gossiping. I never spoke to them unless I had to. The tightest bunch of bastards I have ever met. Never shared their grub or their mugs of tea. Or their cash if you were skint. And they never offered you a cigarette. Then if you bought them a drink they thought you were off your rocker and also resented it because they were obliged to buy you one back and never did, so that was them marked as miserable in their own estimation, not because they thought it but because you did, or so they thought. But they thought wrong. I could not have cared less.

I just did it to flummox them. In their opinion city folk were either thieves or simpletons. An amazing shower of crackpots the lot of them.

The barmaid in this local pub was a daughter of the village. I think she must have hated me because I represented outside youth – otherwise how come. Apart from myself there were no other single men of her age in the dump. She was chaste I think unless the Irishman ever got there which I doubt. I never fancied her in the first place. A bit tubby. Just if I had not tried I thought the regulars might have felt insulted – the barmaid was not good enough etcetera for a city slicker like me. The night I made the attempt was awful. It reminds me of B feature imitation Barbara Stanwyck films.

Once or twice the manager used to bolt the doors and allow a few regulars to stay behind after closing time. Probably he done it more than that but never when I was there. This time he must have forgotten about me till there I was coming back from the cludgie round the back of the bar to find the shutters drawn, I was locked in. I had been away for ages right enough. That country nighttime comes down like a blanket and I could not find the damn trough thing, plus you had to be careful with the ditches. I saw the manager looking daggers at me but too late now and he had to serve me a pint. It was that local splosh stuff I was drinking. A couple of the same later, and with the local constable in the middle of his own second or third I for some reason threw an arm about the barmaid's waist for which I was dealt an almighty clout on the jaw. What a fist she had on her. I was so amazed I tried to land her one back but missed and fell across the table where the constable was sitting, knocking the drink over his uniform trousers. I was ejected.

Long after midnight, maybe as late as two in the morning, I came back to apologise if anyone was still about, and also to collect the carry-out I had planked in one of the ditches round the back. I had been wandering about retching for ages because of that country wine they had been feeding me. Powerful stuff. Inside the pub the lights had been dimmed but I knew they were still there. I could hear music coming faintly from the lounge. I crept round the side of the building then up on my toes and peering in through the corner of the frosted glass I spied the barmaid there giving it a go as the stripper. Yes. Doing a strip show on top of the lounge bar watched by the copper, the manager and one or two regulars, including an unhealthy old guy called Albert Jenkinson who worked alongside me on the farm. And all silent while they watched. Not a smile amongst them. Even the drink was forgotten. Just the quick drag on the smoke.

I lost my temper at first then felt better, then again lost my temper and had to resist caving in the window and telling them to stick the countryside up their jacksie.

No one noticed me. I did not stay very long. Her body was far too dumpy for a stripper and her underwear was a bit old-fashioned. Her father worked as a gardener in the local nursery and rarely went into the pub.

Once I got my wages the following week, and it was safe, I got off my mark and took the tent with me.

An Enquiry Concerning Human Understanding

During a time prior to this a major portion of my energy was devoted to recollection. These recollections were to be allowed to surface only for my material benefit. Each item dredged was to have been noted as the lesson learned so that never again would I find myself in the situation effected through said item. A nerve wracking affair. And I lacked the discipline. Yet I knew all the items so well there seemed little point in dredging them up just to remember them when I in fact knew them so well already. It was desirable to take it along in calm, stately fashion; rationalizing like the reasonable being. This would have been the thing. This would have been for the experience. And I devoted real time to past acts with a view to an active future. The first major item dredged was an horse by the name of Bronze Arrow which fell at the Last in a novice hurdle race at Wincanton for Maidens at Starting. I had this thing to Eighty Quid at the renumerative odds of eleven-double-one-to-two against. Approaching the Last Bronze Arrow is steadily increasing his lead to Fifteen Lengths ... Fallen at the Last number two Bronze Arrow. This type of occurrence is most perplexing. One scarcely conceives of the ideal method of tackling such an item. But: regarding Description; the best Description of such an item is Ach, Fuck that for a Game.

Afterword

This collection was my contribution to *Lean Tales* alongside the work of Alasdair Gray and Agnes Owens. The book went out of print a few years ago. The original hardback was Alasdair's design although the font we used, Gill Sans, was my suggestion. This and Times Roman, as I recall, were the most common fonts in ordinary jobbing work; in constant production, scrapped after every printing.

I was an apprentice compositor for a short period in the printing trade of fifty years ago. One of my chores was the distribution of less common fonts back into their individual cases. Each letter and letter-space was its own tiny piece of type and in certain fonts, for example Spartan, 6 point 'spaced' was a popular type-face on business-card headings; 'spaced' meant that tiny slivers of lead separated each letter which itself was a sliver of lead. These tiny pieces of type had to be distributed back into their rightful compartments in a font cupboard. A boy's nimble fingers made the job less troublesome. Journeymen's fingers were thicker and found the work more difficult.

Gill Sans is not a typeface myself or anyone else would favour generally for bookwork. In this occasion I thought it might work well. Alasdair agreed and Agnes was leaving the matter to us, so we went ahead.

Other than that Alasdair did everything, as many versions and varieties of versions as were necessary. I met with him one afternoon up in his old Kersland Street flat to conclude the decision-making process. At the risk of sentimentalising the occasion, I had brought a half bottle of uisque. Alasdair had a full yin. He sketched and did paste-ups as we went, checking the colours and colour combinations. The finished result is near perfect. It is a sumptuous book. Short story collections can be 'sumptuous'. I enjoy holding the *Lean Tales* hardback, the sight and smell of it, Alasdair's drawings, his design and graphics, his and Agnes's stories.

It was a surprise to me when Jonathan Cape Ltd., an imprint of Random House, remaindered the book. Their decision coincided with the sale of the French rights. I am glad to say that Lean Tales continues to exist as Histoires Maigres, and may be read in French. In English the collection has been broken irrevocably. Alasdair's 'Lean third' became part of his collected stories while Agnes included her 'Lean third' in her Complete Short Stories published by Polygon Books in 2008. She was then into her eighties.

In October 2014 Agnes died. She was a wonderful writer and we were friends for more than thirty five years. I see her strength as a female strength. It is there in the characters who inhabit her fictions. It is not that these women are survivors, and many do not survive, but they engage in a struggle which is virtually insurmountable. They fight tooth and claw towards an end. This 'end' is taken for granted by a society that expects them to do likewise and punishes them when they don't. This 'end' is the survival, health and well being of their children and young people. In all the time I knew her she lacked the freedom to explore her art with consistency of practice. Those in a position to support her through the public purse failed to act. She never seemed "to qualify". Yet against the odds she created an art that will endure. Her best stories are on a par with any.

In different circumstances all but one of my original 'Lean Third' would have been chapters in an early novel. I was working on four novels during the 1970s, and finished two: *The Busconductor Hines*, was published in 1983 and *A Chancer* a year later. The third was my shot at a Glasgow-based detective story which had the working title, 'The Dear Departed Ideals of Brother Charlie'. The central character was the usual Chandleresque cool dude with working-class roots; this one based in Glasgow. The influential and inimitable Eddie Boyd had established the genre in his radio drama of the 1950s then later in the television series *The View from Daniel Pike*, in which Boyd's world-weary detective was brought to life by Roddy MacMillan.

The novelist Jeff Torrington and myself used to have a laugh about parodying the genre although we never got round to it. There again, Jeff left an unfinished novel when he died and some of that would fit. In my early story a young man lately returned from Australia discovers his elder brother has been killed and sets out to discover the truth. Then he goes on to set up a wee kind of radical detective agency where all manner of local anarchists drop in for a chat. I quite enjoyed working on the story but lacked the will to take it beyond 20-25,000 words. I was in my mid through late twenties at the time, using a heavy old typewriter and with no paper to spare. I made each page do its work; nay margins or line spacing or any such wasteful devices: thirty words squeezed into a line and each line doubled. I could barely re-read a page let alone revise it properly.

Most of my writing energy went into another 'novel', which was untitled and forever unfinished. I broke it up and published sections as short stories from 1972 onwards. The only section ever published as "an extract from an unfinished novel" appeared around 1972 in a wee publication known as *Ashphalt Garden*. This was produced by a collective of young people interested in art and ideas, based in somebody's kitchen in Athole Gardens, in the west end of Glasgow. They held a few meetings and reading events and I can remember going to one, perhaps two. The musician and actor, Allan Tall, did the graphics for the publication. We had not known each other before then, although we attended the same school. Allan was then married to Ann Thomson, a fine poet. I wrote a play for him, *The Busker*. This play derives from the story <u>Old Holborn</u>, which was a section from the untitled novel in progress.

I published other sections or episodes as short stories from this period onwards. It was never written as an ordinary novel in any chronological sense, from a point in time beginning through a middle towards an end. Formally it was exacting. Generally a first person narrator will recount a story that happened in the past. I was developing a first party narrator placed at the centre of the action. This central character was an itinerant worker; an anonymous young man who wanders about taking jobs when he needs them, sleeping where he can. The drama was not only physical but psychological, concerning states of mind; dreams, reflections, whatever. The writing demanded not only time but consistency of practice. There is the need for work but most crucially is the need for sustained work. This requires time and like most ordinary working people I rarely had any to spare. I was too busy working at jobs that drained me of energy, intellectual as well as physical.

If I woke in the morning with work in mind then I rose and worked, no matter how early. It was part of my solitary training and I still operate this way. I realised I was better off doing my writing <u>before</u> I went to work. I developed the habit. One of the worst things for myself when I was driving buses was having to leave the writing to rush out to work. It was always a last minute scramble and if I was late it was assumed I had slept in, whereas I would have been working on my own stuff for the past couple of hours.

Thoughts of work-in-progress kept me going through these hours out on the road, driving from a and arriving at b, wondering how I had got there — my mind away, way way away: short stories, long stories, interconnected stories; stories that were plays, stories that were essays, essays that were stories.

I deliberately avoided thinking about stories-in-progress. If I thought about them too much I might "write them in my head" as opposed to the page. I did not want to do that. The substance of my own stories is the working-through process. I had to keep this 'process' for the page, otherwise the story would not come to exist.

While revising the story <u>O jesus, here come the dwarfs</u> for this new edition I heard Jeff Torrington laugh. Jeff died in 2008. He read an early version in manuscript form, around 1980. He is the one of the few ever to have offered a comment on this story. He said he hadn't a clue what it was about but was chortling while telling me that, as he had while reading it. And I was chortling while he was talking, as I had chortled during the writing and revision process. It is not irrelevant to mention that in the 1950s and 1960s, when the British military was stationed in Germany, members of a certain Scottish battalion were known as the 'Poison Dwarfs'. The reasons surrounding this are debatable, and the occasion of continuing controversy. My story has nothing to do with that, given that the two fellows who destroy the central character's peaceful life in the 'foreign campsite' happen to be Glaswegian, just like himself.

The first part of my early novel *A Chancer* makes use of an old Asbestos and Rubberworks factory in Ruchill Street, Maryhill. This bordered along the Forth & Clyde Canal. It was in this factory in the north of Glasgow that a guy told me the yarn that became the story <u>Acid</u>. He told it to me in the anecdotal form about a guy who used to work beside his uncle. I found it difficult making a story from it. I worked on various versions, some two or three pages in length, before finally it became what it is. That and another canal have been important in my work. This other is one I knew from my days in Manchester: in this instance Salford where I worked in a copper mill for a while. I was on permanent nightshift there. One of the guys worked out of doors and smoked dope. He had a place where he sat staring down the canal; tall factory walls backed onto either side of it. He murmured the same thing to me each night I passed, gesturing along the canal and upwards, Scary jock, scary… I passed him slowly, pushing bogies full of coal that I did not want toppling into the so-called water. My gaffer would have made me dive in after them. My story <u>A Nightboilerman's notes</u> derives from the experience, and would have been a central episode of the untitled novel.

I began factory life at the age of fifteen and three months. Over the years I heard a few working stories. I hoped to collect and write some down in inventive ways, create others completely: publish the whole as a book. This would have been influenced particularly by the speculative short prose of Franz Kafka, Gertrude Stein and Jorge Luis Borges. I had been reading Kafka since my teens; in my mid twenties I came upon two wonderful collections by Stein, both published by Black Sparrow Press: *Volumes I and II of the previously uncollected writings: Reflection on the Atomic Bomb* [1973] and *How Writing is Written* [1974]. Black Sparrow published some interesting prose fiction in the 1970s, beginning from Charles Bukowski but including Fielding Dawson.

Dawson was the only fiction writer to attend Black Mountain College. Of contemporary writers he was one I would have enjoyed talking with about writing, and I did meet him once, then corresponded briefly. He began as a visual artist and his eye for a story was aided by that. Dawson remains an underrated writer. It is disappointing that hardly anybody in the States seems to know his work. Bukowski was exciting too, and perhaps more fun but never as crucial a voice for myself. I was more interested in stuff that might extend the form and Bukowski's first party narratives were not in that league, not that I could see. Yet some of his tales made me laugh aloud, and Dawson's never managed that. It aint a competition. I liked them both.

Jorge Luis Borges was doing something radical in a different way. His *Book of Imaginary Beings* had been in my possession since 1971-72. My project on factory tales was influenced strongly by it. Apart from Acid others were The Hon, A Rolling Machine and The Habits of Rats. The last two I also had earmarked for the untitled novel.

My first collection of stories, *An Old Pub Near the Angel* was published in 1973 and contains sections of the untitled novel, including the title story. In 1976 *Three Glasgow Writers* appeared. Tom Leonard and Alex Hamilton were the other two. My contribution included the stories

The City Slicker and the Barmaid, and Where I Was, episodes from the same untitled novel. When this book was remaindered a few short years later we three writers received some 70 copies each. I still have most of mine. I piled them high and scrawled in a black felt-tip marker: What A Load Of Shite – not in reference to the book itself but the entire literary enterprise. Then I continued work.

I published many sections from this 'novel-in-progress' in the early years. These were stories in their own right and if not I made them so. But I was drifting away from the original project. Nuances of character distinguished one narrator from another. There were inconsistencies. Things were just not right. What was missing was consistency of practice. I could have rectified the problems with adequate time. But I did not have the time; the usual problem and it drove me nuts.

I grudged any time away from my typewriter. Worse than that. If I could not write what would become of me? Leastways my head might explode. Roughly speaking, life was inconceivable. I needed that day-to-day working practice otherwise I knew it would fail, my writing would fail, I knew it would, everything, all the short stories and plays and so-called 'novels in progress', my entire work as a whole, it would never fulfil whatever it had to fulfil for it to succeed in the manner I thought that it could, that I needed. I needed to be doing what these other artists were doing. It rankled with me that I was unable to do my work, and I wanted to confront all these shit journalists, crap reviewers and mean-spirited academics who persist in scorning those who shout or embody the truth, that art cannot be sustained by wage-slaves, by people whose time on this planet is sold as the means to survival whether of them or their families.

I considered giving up full-time employment altogether. But what if I did? The State beats down our humanity. One way they do it is to make resigning from wage-slavery very awkward indeed. In those days it meant thirteen weeks without unemployment benefit. One needed another job to walk straight into: or else money in the bank, or a partner who earned money, or a family who kept you going economically. If none of that applied you sought welfare benefit from the Department of Social Security [DSS] which was the situation facing most people. I was used to unemployment as a single man, scratching about, but when children come along it makes the difference.

By 1977 I was involved in The Print Studio Press, a writers' cooperative. We thought to produce our own good quality pamphlets, mainly work that nobody else would publish. Within a reasonably short period of time, aside from my *Short Tales from the Nightshift*, we produced *Forwords*, Tom Buchan; *Islands*, Liz Lochhead; *If only Bunty was here*, Tom Leonard; *Muthos for Logos*, James Taylor; *The Comedy of the White Dog*, Alasdair Gray; *Glasgow Zen*, Alan Spence; *The One-legged Tapdancer*, Carl McDougall and *Imaginary Wounds*, Aonghas Macneacail. We were to be doing further titles by Tom McGrath and Brian McCabe but by then our publishing operation petered out. Six of these ten little stories in my Print Studio Press pamphlet derive from sections lifted from this never-finished novel.

I had become acquainted with the poet Stewart Conn and his wife Judy; our weans had attended the same pre-school playgroup. Stewart was working for the BBC at that time and was an enthusiastic, generous man, and an advocate of contemporary writing, responsible for broadcasting the work of contemporary writers. He had wanted to broadcast my story <u>Remember Young Cecil</u>. The problem was that the language would have had to be revised, in one instance only. If not the BBC was unable to broadcast. I had a look at the cause of the bother, that particular 'bad' word, but found it impossible to subsitute any other word at all, never mind one that was 'good'. The character who speaks in 'bad' language hardly opens his mouth at all in this story. He would have died of lung failure had I wrenched the words out his mouth to suit the BBC authorities.

I withdrew that story and submitted another, a section from my novel-in-progress entitled <u>The Block</u>. The night it was broadcast by the BBC I sat there listening to the opening sentences. Out came this extraordinary upper-middle class anglocentric RP bastard of a voice that murdered my first person narrator. I switched off the radio and avoided jumping out the window. Ironically the actor was Scottish. Like every other UK actor with 'an accent' he was forced 'to lose his voice' to work for the BBC, those guardians of High English Culture who will commandeer the very nails from your fingers and show amazement if you offer resistance.

An English anthology, *Firebird*, edited by Tim Binding for Hamish Hamilton Ltd. included a story of mine in 1981, another episode from the never-finished novel. This one was entitled <u>not not while the giro</u> and became the title of my next collection of short stories. The £200 advance was utter shite but I always liked the book. For the cover design we used a drawing by John Taylor, a fine artist and a friend. By coincidence Alasdair Gray's *Unlikely Stories Mostly* was published in the same month, February 1983. We held a joint launch party at the old Third Eye Centre on Sauchiehall Street. A very cheery occasion.

At least twelve of the stories contained in my *Not Not While the Giro* collection were part of my novel-in-progress. This publication changed matters. I had to admit an unwelcome truth. It was no longer conceivable that I might draw all the finished and unfinished sections together, and render a whole with the necessary consistency and coherence, such that I might call it a novel.

The title story of the collection, <u>not not while the giro</u>, was pivotal in my original conception of the novel. The central character has returned to where he had been living before, and meditates on leaving once again. This section would operate at the end or midway through the novel. Midway through was the more likely, separating Scottish locations from elsewhere. In the section to follow the character would appear in altered circumstances. This would mirror the technical leap from the static reflective narrative, into a 'new reality', a dynamic place where first party narrators exist at the heart of the drama as it occurs. The title itself and its use of the double negative was also my attempt to present the case, that even at the lowest economic level people live their lives, in spite of State or societal intervention.

Even without the restrictions in time I might never have finished that novel. No, I do not believe that. I would have finished it. It failed through no fault of my own.

From the dregs of that never-finished novel I created a large number of short stories and these have appeared in each of my short story collections. My first published collection *An Old Pub Near the Angel* has about five of these or possibly six; *Short Tales from the Nightshift* has five, possibly six; *Three Glasgow Writers* has two. The 1983 publication, *Not Not While the Giro* includes the title story itself, and a further nine or ten, excluding two that appear in *An Old Pub Near the Angel*. In *Greyhound for Breakfast* there are about eight; *The Burn* has two, I think. In *The Good Times* there are at least two. And in my last collection, *If It Is Your Life* believe it or not, there are two, or is it three? Who knows what else is lying around.

Yet the largest number of these stories were brought together here in my third of the original *Lean Tales*. All bar one of the eighteen stories was to be a section of that novel. This one exception is the story <u>Are you drinking sir?</u> whose first person narrator is a man in his 60s, from eastern Europe. I used to think of him as 'elderly'; now that I am into my 60s I see he is not so elderly after all, he might even be 'youngish'.

James Kelman
December 2014

april 2015

This first edition is published

as a trade paperback; there are 100 numbered

and lettered copies signed by the author and handbound

in boards by Tangerine Press, Tooting, London; the copies

lettered K, E, L, M, A and N are additionally

housed in a custom slipcase.